Knock, Knock!

It's Your

Enemy Boss

J.P. Sterling

UpCycling My Rig-Pig Boss

© copyright 2023 J.P. Sterling

Editors: Rebecca Carpenter and Brenda Bastien

Proofreader: Samantha Pottie

CONTENTS

Author's Note

Dear Reader,

This book was previously published as *Upcycling My Rig-Pig Boss*. While I loved that title, I quickly realized the slang wasn't familiar to most readers. With this new title and cover update, I've also added a brand-new extended epilogue that shares Beau and Clover's a-year-after marriage. I hope you enjoy the glow-up—and the new title too!

Thank you for being the best reader community ever.

One

CLOVER

"Well, you can't spell funeral without fun." I stared at the busy downtown street from my tiny office window while doing my best to divert Charlotte's question about how my weekend had gone. My soft-spoken coworker stood behind me, following me like a lost puppy. Turning back to her, I pulled up one side of my lips into the only grin I could manage in a desperate attempt to try to appear neutral to my imploding life.

"It's okay, Clover." Charotte gently squeezed my forearm, like she was both unsure of what to do, but also wanted to fill in for the loving mother I had just lost. "No one expects you to enjoy this. You don't have to pretend not to be sad."

Charlotte had been tip toeing around me, like she was expecting me to crack at any moment. She didn't know I was an expert at masking my emotions. I was the last person to cry—especially in front of someone—even when I was dying inside. "It's cool." I moved away from the window, taking steps around my upcycled-door desk—and the sympathy pot of succulents that Charlotte had brought me—toward the door.

I had done my duty, working a full eight hours the day after I had buried my mother. It's cliché to say she was too young to die, but really at sixty-five, she had so much life left to live. As much as I tried to explain that to anyone who would listen, it didn't matter, and I couldn't change it. I swept my eyes to my sister, Poppy, while I dug deep—like way down deep to my toes—for the strength not to cry out in overwhelming grief for the mother I had lost, and the new caregiver role I was now being forced to fill. It was officially time to start my new normal.

Charlotte's head tipped to Poppy, who sat crossed legged on the floor, doing nothing other than hugging her stuffed pig and humming to herself. "Have you thought of what you are going to do with your sister?"

Halting my steps, my eyes met hers. "I have thought about it."

"And?"

I was patient with myself while I forced down the lump in my throat, my words tumbled out in a whisper, "And this world stinks."

Charlotte's words were equally as soft, "Care to elaborate?"

No. I screamed inside, because I had always been a private person who prided myself on leaving my personal life at home. I'd had an impossible week, now forced to bring my sister *with* me. As respectful as Charlotte was of Poppy being here, she had to be curious, and hoping I had a better plan. Letting out a sigh of defeat, I reluctantly replied, "There isn't much to say. As you are aware, she's not capable of staying alone. She's nineteen, way too old for daycare, but her disability isn't the right fit for any of the group homes in town. Even if it was a good fit, none of them have availability on short notice. I talked to a lady at the county social services office, and she suggested I could move her to a different county where they had room. I understand that their hands are tied, but moving her away from me right after she lost her mom seems cruel. I can't afford to stay home like my mom did. Mom had been retired, not to mention she had the patience of a saint."

Charlotte's gaze was soft, and filled with empathy. "What *are* you going to do?"

Chewing my lip softly, I wracked my brain. I imagine it would have helped if I had gotten more than a handful of hours of sleep in the last week. I was numb to it all, everything from my emotions, to the funeral arrangements, and that wasn't me. I had always been a planner. I always had ideas. Today I was in a mental void. Tossing my shoulder, I spoke my words as I thought them, "Short-term solution, I found a lady down the street who watches kids and is willing to take her, starting Monday. It's not really her thing, and she's charging me double the normal rate, which will deplete most of my paycheck. She also only agreed to do it short term, so I need to come up with a better long-term solution."

"Double?" Her brows raised toward me. "Is that legal?"

"I could question her, but I was insanely lucky to find anyone on such short notice."

"Right." Charlotte nodded gently. "It's like she needs a specialized day center with other adults who are more her peers. Too bad you can't open one of your own."

"Wait a second." My eyes shifted from side to side as I ran her words over in my mind a few times. I don't know why I didn't think about that before. People start day centers all the time. What's to stop me from opening one with an older target clientele?

"Oh, no—" Charlotte's voice ticked up a notch. "I see that look in your—."

"It's perfect!" I cut her off. "I can totally do this for her."

"Are you sure it's not too much of a project to take on?" Her voice lowered respectfully, hinting at bad news. "That sounds like a full-time job. You would need special training, and you have your full-time job here, and now you're a full-time caregiver for Poppy, and—"

"I don't have a choice and I can hire someone with the training," I interrupted her again, already pulling out my phone to look up government regulations. "I have to work, and I can't afford to keep her where she is now. If I set up a center, I can get grants to help pay for her care. I mean, I must at least try." I opened my internet browser, ready to type in my search words when my screen flashed an emergency news article that instantly made me sick to my stomach. "Texas oil drilling company owner and CEO responds to deep-sea well explosion."

"What's this about?" I asked as I clicked on the window to open a live video feed.

Charlotte leaned in. "What are you talking about?"

"There's a well explosion?" My eyes raised to her momentarily, before returning to the video. My heart rate ticked up a notch, adding to my already sickened gut feeling. "Did you know about this?

Charlotte was quiet for too long, giving away her knowledge of the event, before she answered timidly, "It flashed across my screen a few minutes ago."

I bit my lip, assuming the reason she hadn't said anything was because I was already stressed out. I also didn't have anyone blowing up my phone, and I could only assume everyone else on the planet was protecting me right now, too. I didn't need to be protected. I was going to live. The planet, on the other hand, needed an advocate, and I was doing my best to do my part. More than my part, it was my entire life's purpose to fight for this planet. I took a lot of pride in my work with green companies. Just last year I was awarded the Green Business Award for my work in specializing in green PR. Having an environmental disaster such as this—right in my own backyard—was definitely something I needed to know about.

Charlotte and I watched as the video zoomed in over the gulf waters. Oil floated on the Gulf, darkening what should have been clear water. A rippling noise cut through the video, and when they zoomed out, I could see the noise belonged to a helicopter closing in on the shore, lowering for a landing. The heading on the screen read: Tucker Drilling CEO, Beau Tucker. I blurted out, "You have got to be kidding me."

"What?" Charlotte's eyes locked back on me.

"This was a Tucker well? And that nasty CEO has the gall to pull up onto the beach in his private helicopter like he hasn't already banked enough carbon under his footprint." I turned my head away from the screen, fully appalled. *Some people just didn't get it, and never would!*

"Wait," Charlotte started, "is that the same guy who had a land spill last summer?"

"Same filthy man." Shaking my head, I didn't have anything else to add. There wasn't anyone greedier than him. He clearly did anything he could to make more money for himself, without a care in the world for what he was doing to the planet. I closed out my internet browser as I couldn't stomach it. "If Ebenezer Scrooge had a twin, it'd be Beau

Tucker. He'd be called *Beau*nezer Scrooge. I'm just relieved
I can close him out of my browser."

I tucked my phone into my bag, not able to say anything about this current event. It seemed to be the icing
on my-week-stinks calendar. Picking up Poppy's favorite
hemp-crocheted purse, I handed it to her, and helped her
off the floor while saying to Charlotte, "I'll deal with this
tomorrow. Right now, I need to go home to spend some
quality time with Poppy."

Two

BEAU

I was busy as a cat on a hot tin roof as I flew my helicopter back to my shop. I had returned from checkin' my well, and the sight of the oil on the beach, and the poor birds left me physically weak. It wasn't the first time I'd had this kind of mess. The silver lining I clung to today was, all my guys were safe. In this job, I'd learned to put things into perspective, and people—my people—were the first and only thing that mattered.

This wasn't the best place to land—a mere clearin' in a field out by my shop—but in times like these, I couldn't waste time in traffic. Angling my helicopter's nose into the wind, I scanned the field, and saw clearly what I had already figured. Protesters around my shop. I wasn't at all surprised, but the sight of them sent a wave of jitters to my gut. They were un-avoidable since I was 'bout out of fuel. I was careful about my ground effect. The wind was blowin' so hard that I reckoned I'd bounce, and I sure didn't want to hit anyone. I turned the throttle down to an even idle, and I sat there 'bout a foot above ground, not wantin' to land. I could see their screaming faces, and their painted protect-the-earth signs, and they were comin' for me. I definitely needed to get a private landing dock, something with a high gate and security. Some of these hippies would get violent, and all I wanted was to do my job. I didn't plan any of this disaster. It came with the gig. Gulping down my anxiety, I closed the gap of air, safely landing my copter.

Now the hard part. People.

Mad people, swarmin' like fire ants who'd had their hill demolished. It was like they had blinders on, and didn't fear for their safety as they plowed toward my copter while the blades were still turning. One guy stepped up to my door, pressed his face against the glass, and pounded a fist at me. *This was out of control!* I had to do something before someone got hurt. I didn't even know how I could open my door with the people crowding in, pushin' and shovin'. I could sleep in the helicopter, but something told me they'd still be here in the mornin'. Defeated, I did the only thing I could do. I panicked and called the cops for help.

It'd been years since I got hauled home in the backseat of a cop car, and it brought back so many memories of my rowdier high school days. I liked to think I'd learned a little since those humble beginnings. Now, it was well past midnight, and the street was quiet. The only sound was Bandit's paws bouncin' off my screen door, as he jumped around waitin' for my arrival.

"Sorry, Boy." I carefully opened the door, so it didn't smack him. "I got caught up at work again. I bet you're hungry as a horse."

Runnin' in circles, he followed me to the kitchen where I filled his bowl with dog food and set it on the floor. It was a rare night he didn't share some cooked meat with me, but it was too late for this ol' dog to hunt. As tired as I was, I wouldn't be able to sleep. I didn't even risk closing my eyes, as the images of my crew having to endure this disaster chewed at my stomach. Not to mention the colossal cost of cleanup I'd have to fund—I wasn't complaining about that part because I got lucky and nobody'd died—but I still owed it to my investors to somehow turn a profit. I couldn't imagine having to lay off people after this. That would kill me, because most my guys had families and they were the ones out there riskin' their lives.

No, sleep was not on the menu. Instead, I went to my garage, to tinker on my new-to-me pinball machine. A1947 Humpty Dumpty pinball machine, with all original flippers and fittin's. Runnin' my hand along the wood, I remembered the vintage green, red and gold color pattern. I played this same model of pinball machine all through middle school, while I waited at the diner for my mom to get off work. Another scan over the body, and I determined all she needed was a new rubber kit and some bulbs and she'd be ready to play again. I loved restoring these things. What most people thought was old and ugly, I saw as well-loved and worth it. They were easy to fix too.

Not at all like people. Ugh, now I was thinking about people again. Mad and upset people who hated me. I'd been a loner my whole life. Teased for being ugly, I stopped tryin' to belong. Maybe that's why I was able to tolerate people hatin' me for the job I did? It made me a billionaire but, it didn't make me all that happy. In the beginning, I loved what I did because I was good at it, but now, it made me a prisoner.

Backing away from the pinball machine, I shut off the overhead garage light, and went into the house to find my bottle of Mylanta, all while promising to myself something had to change. I couldn't let this get so out of hand that people get hurt, nor could I rely on the police to give me a ride home every night. I had an obligation to do the best I could for my company—my guys—and for myself. Tomorrow, I was gonna do something different. Somethin' I hated doing. I was gonna to ask someone for help.

Three

CLOVER

My brows skyrocketed and my words sputtered resembling an old carburetor that wouldn't turn over. "I-I know you! You're th-that horrible man from the news! You're—"

"Beau Tucker." He extended his burly arm, offering a handshake, and held it there in pause while I stared at it like it was covered in snake venom. I triple-blinked, trying to find the connection. For the life of me, I couldn't fathom why this scum would land in my office.

Not wanting to show weakness, I swallowed my distaste, and briefly gripped his hand, and held my breath. He was such a filthy mess, you'd think a billionaire could at least shower and put on clothes that didn't look slept in. I struggled to keep my polite composure when I asked, "What are you doing here?"

"I need your help—"

I pushed my hand out in the perfect stop signal. "Not a chance."

"Hold your little hippie horses," his thick Texas drawl rolled out. "The oil and gas industry has gotten a bad reputation for being environmentally unfriendly, but I really do think it's a media problem, more than anything. The media has gone all cattywampus and I want my company to be a leader in changing the image of the entire industry. I know you specialize in greenin' things up, and you can help me out of this predicament."

I was still so stunned he would show up in my office uninvited, I started acting out of character, and not at all like my normal, welcoming self. I didn't have any desire to be nice to him. I haughtily tossed a lock of my golden hair over my shoulder and forced my face into a neutral expression, like I was clearing a slate. "Flattery won't work with me."

"I wasn't tryin' to flatter ya." He went stone-faced, steeling his chin. "I was tryin' to pay ya."

"I have a full client load right now." I motioned to the digital calendar on my computer screen, doing my best to sound bored with him, and used the opportunity to take a step back, away from the rig-pig stench emanating from his aura. "If I took you on, I wouldn't be able to give you the time your account would need." I stared at him, biting back the truth, which was I'd rather clean up dog poop all day than even have to look at this man.

One of his greasy locks of hair dropped down onto this forehead, dangling there like its sole purpose was to gross me out. I was so utterly repulsed by this man, I barely heard his firm rebuttal, "I'll give ya a hundred thousand dollars."

"Wait a second." I nervously tugged my hair back over my shoulder, doubting I had heard him correctly. "What amount was that?"

His eyes shifted, like he suspected he had hit my *let's-make-a-deal* nerve. "I'll sign a contract for one-hundred thousand dollars if you agree to make all this drama disappear."

I tried to avoid choking as I swallowed. I dropped my eyes to the floor, noticing his worn steel-toed boots, and the trail of mud they'd left on my newly installed bamboo floor. One side of my brain was begging me to ask, if he had that much money to throw around, why he didn't invest in at least one clean pair of shoes for those days he showed up in people's offices? He was clearly loaded. I worked on a fifty percent commission rate, and I quickly did the math, confirming he was offering me as much money as I made with all my other clients combined.

However, the other side of my brain flashed a warning sign that said don't be fooled. This guy ran one of the most corrupt oil companies in the business. No amount of my green PR expertise could ever make a dent in his bad image. These guys oozed filth from their core.

My brain was waging a war in me, pulling me to think about the money again. This would give me the money I needed to pay for Poppy's care while I took the time to start an adult day center, and boy, would that save everything. I took a deep measured breath, as if I was getting ready to jump off the high dive, because it hurt to say no to that amount of money. "I'm sorry, Mr. Tucker. I don't think our companies are the right fit for a partnership. I wish—"

He kept his chin lifted, and his body straight like a soldier in line when he upped his offer, "Two hundred and fifty."

Now I did choke, and one hand flew to my throat as I bobble headed my way through breathing, while my other hand floundered behind me, grasping for the edge of my desk. I needed to lean on something to avoid collapsing. "You sure know how to give a girl a heart attack, don't you?"

"I don't know nothin' bout heart attacks, but that possum's on a stump."

"What possum?" I deadpanned, equal parts confused and stunned. There was no way I could look at this greedy, nasty, grumpy man and ever want to help him. My conscience wasn't allowing me to say yes, but I was left asking myself at what cost did it make it okay to accept the job and say, "It's just business?"

Helping this troll went against everything I believed in. Still, there was something else I believed in—helping my disabled sister. And that much money would help us through this tough financial season until I had the center opened. I wasn't kidding myself with this center project. It was going to take time. All that time meant I was going to be spending thousands on sending Poppy to the lady down the street, and I didn't have the funds to do that. At some point in the near future, I'd have to make serious lifestyle changes to continue spending that amount of money. I'd either lose my apartment, or be forced into a weekend job. Either way, I didn't want to ditch Poppy in her time of grief. My head was spinning, weighing all the consequences of what I potentially had to lose by leaving this offer on the table. With my brows bunched together like two mis-matched socks that had been tumbled together in the dryer, I glared at him. "Why did you come to me?"

His eyes caught mine, and although I had expected them to be beady, like the most disgusting reptilian creature, they weren't. They were soft, with natural hues of warm and cozy browns, like one of those wrinkly puppy dogs. They widened when he spoke, like he was laying down all his cards. "I've seen you on the news and people love you. I feel in my gut that I can trust you on this."

A knot budded in my stomach, knowing this was a dangerous idea, but two-hundred and fifty thousand dollars . . . "You do realize this is nearly impossible?" Even though I had asked the question, it seemed more like a last-ditch effort to talk myself out of this awful idea.

"That's why I came to you." His voice was gruff, like when I'd heard him speak on the news, but it wasn't unkind, making me want to believe him.

The media only presented one side of the story, and they sensationalized things to sell their stories. My job was to show the other side, and I was good at my job. He was right. If there was anyone who could help change his image, it would be me.

It was an awful lot of money at stake. What if it really could be mine? If I agreed to help him, I could change both of our lives. I could help Poppy, but there was even more to consider. This PR mess was at a global level. If I could turn it around—and get all the credit for it—that would be super-impressive to my boss. I could get a promotion—perhaps even partner—which would put me in an even better position to improve my, and Poppy's, lives forever. It was as tempting as dark chocolate in a health food store. "So," I started in an inquiring tone, trying one last time to see if he was genuinely being sincere. "Would you agree to do whatever I tell you to do? I can't handle any stubbornness or pushback because it's already almost impossible."

His eyes were unflinching when he agreed. "Whatever it takes."

I paced in front of him, stating my conditions as they came to me, praying this wasn't a mistake. "We will start with a thirty-day trial period. If, for any reason, I decide that I can't continue working the remainder of the contract, I will be able to walk away clean."

"Deal." His hand shot out, waiting for me to shake it again.

Instead, I walked back to my desk. "I don't do handshakes. I need this in writing."

He humbly lowered his hand. "Whatever you need."

"I will have my assistant, Charlotte, draw up the contract, and get it to you by the end of the day. As for starting this project, I will need the rest of the day to research and put together a plan. I'll be in your office first thing tomorrow morning to go over it with you."

He held up his index finger, interjecting. "One question."

I quirked an eyebrow and gave him my best side-angled stare. "What's that?"

"You're not one of those crazy girls who looks up my personal record or anything, are you?"

I didn't flinch because I had gotten this question many times before, and I quickly confirmed, "Oh, yes. I am. I will know everything about you by the time we finish working together, but don't worry. I'll spin everything in your favor."

I half-expected him to start touting back demands of his own, but he held my gaze and simply said, "Thank you."

I hadn't expected a moment like this, something so sincere. Most clients paired me up with their assistants and barely even spoke to me, let alone gave me any thanks. The look in his eyes told me that he was grateful. That scared me. I didn't want him to think this would be easy. We had a lot of work to do. I stared at him without even a hint of a smile. "You won't be thanking me after seeing what I have planned for you."

Four

BEAU

A scuffle alerted me, and I glanced up to see Clover passing through my glass, office door without waiting for an invitation. It didn't take me long to figure out she was one of those girls who said hello with her hips. I blinked, trying not to get distracted, but she was all gussied up in one of those long floral dresses, and had changed the hoop in her nose to a little diamond stud. She spoke like she was making an announcement to an auditorium filled with grade schoolers. "Day one of my thirty-day reputation resurrection plan."

I paused, feeling both intrigued, and slightly ambushed. "I didn't know you were here."

"Now you do." She plopped down on a chair in front of my desk and didn't seem to take a breath when she went on. "I stayed up all night and watched every interview you've given online. You're a mess."

Even though I had the AC cranked, my brow started to bead with sweat at the thought of her watching all of my online interviews. It was like having all your most embarrassing moments in life suddenly exposed all at once. I tugged at my collar, trying to let in some air. "Ah, okay."

"It's not okay." She pointed a sharp finger at me like I was the bad kid in her class. "I made a thirty-day emergency plan, and it starts now."

"Now?" I looked at the paper calendar on my desk, speaking as I read over my appointments, "I have a few meetings this morning."

"This won't take long, and while we're at it"–she reached over, scooping up my desk calendar— "you won't use paper anymore. I'll recycle this for you."

Raising my eyebrows, I spoke with skepticism. "Isn't it more wasteful not to finish using it since I already bought it?"

"Yes, in a sense, but we are cleaning up your image, which starts today." Her words were choppy, as if they were suffering from too much punctuation. "So, no more paper. I'll have my assistant upload your schedule into an electronic one."

"I have an electronic version." I motioned to my phone. "I just like to keep a hard copy in front of me."

She kept a straight face and peered down her perfectly straight nose at me. "Not anymore." That stuck in my throat like hair on a biscuit. I wanted to remind her technology wasn't always reliable, but she had this hyper-spunk thing going on, reminding me of one of those yippy dogs. I decided to let her do her thing before she peed all over me. I wasn't expecting her to act this way when I hired her. Yesterday, she seemed so . . . not like this. I bit my tongue, waiting for her to finish her announcements. "So, number one rule of the plan is never, ever, and I mean ever, talk to the media for . . . eternity."

This was clearly a reference to how the media made me out to be a villain. It was my main concern, and I was glad she addressed this first. Still, I didn't see how not talkin' to them would help as they tended to follow me everywhere I went. "So, what do I do when they get in my face and won't leave?"

"You call me." She leaned forward and spoke with her hands, as if she was explaining things to a small child, making me wonder if she thought I was stupid. "If they corner you on the street or somewhere, with a camera, you call me at that very moment. You literally give your phone to the media, and I will talk to them on camera, so we have our own record. Don't ever talk to anyone in public again."

"I can do that." A wave of relief washed through my gut. This was exactly what I had needed. Maybe not necessarily this much spunk—I could do without the nose ring—but I had desperately wanted someone to deal with all the noise forever. It may seem trivial, but I had been bullied about my looks all my life. I wasn't what you'd call classically good-looking, or even average. You could best describe me as the best-lookin' turd in a punch bowl, and I loathed being in front of the camera. My insecurities take over, and visions of people laughin' at me as they did in grade school swarm around my head, and I can't shut out the noise. I always ended up blurtin' out the most random things, and never the right thing. My relief was short-lived as she went on.

"Rule two." She grabbed my coffee cup and dropped it dramatically into the trash. "You are done with disposables. I only want to see you using reusable everything."

My eyes locked longingly on my cup resting in the trash. "There's still coffee in there."

She lifted her pale-as-paper foot, clad in a hippie sandal, and stuck it on top of the trash, blocking my view with her shoe. "I don't care." Her eye lock was one of those you'd see in fantasy movies between a knight and an evil dragon. She was definitely the dragon, and she looked like she was about to blow smoke right out of her nose. I held my breath as she continued, "Rule three. You give me your passwords to your social media profiles, and you promise never to go on them again."

Another rush of relief, as I hated social media. "That you can have," I said with a cleansing sigh.

"Rule four." She paused, inclining her chin as she looked down at me over her nose again, and I was beginning to see that nose piercing like an exclamation point. Not a good one, either. It was one that screamed danger and don't proceed. It hooked my attention, even more, when she asked, "Do you remember when you said you wouldn't be stubborn?"

I sighed heavily, knowing she was playing some sort of game, but I also was sick of people picketing my office and home. I wanted everything to go away—now! So far, she seemed to have a plan. One I didn't *love*, but it wasn't terrible, so I spoke firmly with conviction, "Yeah, just tell me what it is."

"This one might hurt, but there isn't any way around it."

I wasn't a child, and resented the way she was treatin' me like one. I ran one of the most successful drillin' companies in all of Texas, and I was a hard businessman. I wasn't afraid of something hurtin', but her snarkiness was becoming more annoying than a Bible salesman at a church lock-in. "I'm not going to be stubborn."

"Give me the keys to your monster truck."

I narrowed my eyes, all trust for her going out the window. *Like Sam Hill I will!* In the roughest voice I could muster, I asked, "Why?"

"It has to go." She said it so matter-of-factly, but her facts were messed up.

"Like, storage?" I wasn't necessarily asking, as I already knew the answer. My mama taught me never to say I hated people, but at this point I knew I wouldn't even walk across the street to piss on her if she was on fire.

"You are selling it, and the proceeds are going to your new favorite green charity."

"I don't have a favorite green charity," I retorted in a gruff voice.

She flashed her know-it-all smirk. "I'll find you one."

"How will I get to work?"

She pulled out a small set of keys from her backpack and slid them across my desk. "I got you an electric scooter. Of course, you are getting the bill."

If I had felt a tiny bit of relief before, it had all vanished. Now, a sinking feeling set in my gut. Not only was hiring Clover a bad idea, but I knew her game now. She wasn't about helping me as much as teaching me a lesson. She was one of those young hippies who thought they knew everything.

She stared smugly at me.

But I gave it right back.

She was, in fact, enjoying this.

I hated it, but what choice did I have?

My irritation grew. This hippie didn't even know me. She was like everyone else, and only saw what the media put out there, which was my problem. As much as I wanted to tell her our partnership wasn't going to work, and send her out the door, I understood I was looking at someone who hated me because of my media issue. She was here to fix it, and I didn't see anyone else lining up to help. If she said cleaning up my image would help, what would it hurt to drive a scooter for a few days? Play her game. Change the media's perception of me, and then go buy a bigger, more jacked up truck when this is all over. I dug in my pocket, pulling out my pocketknife, lose change and some gum wrappers before I found my keys. I reluctantly laid the fob on the desk, like I was giving up, because I felt like I was.

Five

CLOVER

Back at my apartment, I stood in the doorway to my living room and zoomed in on the picture I had saved on my phone. A perfect piece of commercial real estate. A friend of mine who worked for the city had alerted me to this precious jewel today, saying it would go to auction by the end of the month. It was a huge step to buy a building but I figured it was the best way forward because I didn't want to risk renting, and setting up everything, only to lose my lease. I was going to do this, and I was going all in. If I could get funding before the end of the month, the city would make a private sale on their building. Beau's offer couldn't have come at a more perfect time. My heart was about to burst with excitement for my sister when I asked her, "What do you think we should name your new center?"

Poppy was sitting in her usual spot on the couch, zoned out on the TV, watching cartoons. She gave me a wrinkled-nose grin, confirming she had heard me, but she didn't answer my question with any audible sound. That was a typical response for her that I took as a good sign.

A text lit up on my phone from my assistant:

Charlotte: "R U watching this?!"

Me: "???"

Charlotte: "UR new client is on the news again. It's bad!"

My eyes popped open like they were spring-loaded as I urgently switched my browser to tune in. It only took me a moment to recognize Beau's greasy mullet talking to Susie from Channel 5, and my throat knotted like a pine tree. Susie was the sort of reporter who made even the most seasoned speakers nervous. Once she found a weak spot, she didn't shy away. Instead, she would dig in like a corkscrew, twisting your words until she got you to say something juicy she could sell. I turned the volume on my phone all the way up and heard Susie ask: "What's your company culture like?"

Beau answered without even so much as a thoughtful pause. "Extremely demanding, competitive, and to be honest, a little vicious."

What is he thinking?

Why is he even talking to her?

I told him no interviews!

I rubbed my forehead and raced to think about how to stop the interview. I would never be able to contact him in time, and he wouldn't answer his phone while on camera. I could call in a fire drill or something, but people generally frowned on that. I nervously paced my small living room, waiting for the horror show to unfold.

Susie: "Do you generally get along with your employees?"

Beau: "Some of them, but some of the others can't stand me because I make them work too hard. This business isn't for snowflakes and wussies."

I lowered my head, slowly shaking it, refusing to watch as listening was hard enough.

Susie: "Are you saying you don't get along with people?"

Beau: "I get on with most people . . . except maybe stupid people."

I squeezed my fists together so hard they were shaking. *He did not just say that!* I wished I had a giant alarm, like the X factor button, that I could pounce on to make him stop. I thought it couldn't get any worse. I was wrong.

Beau: "Can you be done with these dumb questions? I'm tired from being up all night working."

Throwing my hands up, I fought real tears. So much for him agreeing to follow my rules! The guy was a certified jerk. If this is how it is on day one, I need to cut my losses before he drags me down with him. Then, like my heart was ahead of my brain, something in me forced my eyes to land back on

Poppy, and my heart twisted, like it was being wrung out by Beau's greasy hands. I couldn't risk the state stepping in, and moving her to another county when I ran out of money to pay for her care. But could I risk my reputation on a guy who clearly was trying to spite me—test the electric fence to see if I was on it, so to speak? Since he made it obvious, he was testing boundaries, it was time for me to give him a shock to try to right this ship now, or he'd never change.

Cringing, I turned back to the interview. *Please stop! I can't watch anymore.* Thankfully, Susie accepted his request and wrapped up her interview. I paced to my kitchen table which doubled as my home office, pulled out my laptop, and immediately opened every news browser I could. While I waited for the bad news ripple to load, I filled my coffee maker to the top with water and turned it on. It was well after work hours, but I'd be pulling an all-nighter by the time I finished my press release, and handled all the social media backlash.

I honestly didn't know why I cared. Money was money was money. Beau came looking for me. Not the other way around. He could either do what he agreed to do, or find another PR person to dupe. Something niggled at the back of my mind. Maybe he wasn't doing this to spite me, but to test me and to see how good I really was? Either way, it was going to take me all night to clean up this mess.

My hands shook as I reached for my phone, ready to call Beau. I had no idea what I was going to say to him. The look on his face during the interview was passively relaxed. Almost as if he didn't have a clue how bad he was messing up. I'd dealt with PR nightmares before, but this wasn't about what he said. This was more about him blatantly disobeying and not calling me. I was beyond frazzled as I pondered why he would refuse to follow my instructions. There was no way I could be professional with him right now. I set my phone back down and decided to wait until morning, after I had time to cool off.

However, the morning wasn't any better. If anything, having this simmer all night only made me madder. I stormed into his office, being sure to make as much noise as possible, and planted my feet in the center of the room before I declared, "That was disgusting!"

He raised his head from behind his computer. "Pardon me?"

"You!" I pointed at him with a sharp finger. "Last night on the news. I told you NO interviews!"

He rose to his feet, and his voice leveled up a notch to match mine. "I know I did terrible, but where were you?"

I perched a hand on my hip and haughtily answered, "At home, watching and dealing with your social media disaster! I told you no interviews, and now you've created this huge mess! Why didn't you call me?"

"I tried calling, but you never answered your phone!"

"What?" I knew he was lying, but to prove a point, I yanked my phone from my bag, checked it and found no such evidence. "No, you didn't!"

"Yeah, I did. Your phone must not have been working, because I tried calling you about twelve times."

I flashed the screen at him, annoyed he thought he could get away with this lie. "I didn't get any missed calls."

"Let me show you." He grabbed his phone, and before he dialed, he asked, "Make sure I have your number right. Is it 566-5565?"

"Yes," I answered dryly, amazed he was still dragging this excuse out.

He dialed the number and put his phone on speaker, holding it up in the air, and we listened to it ring. My phone didn't light up, or even chime. Then after one ring a voice said, "This number is unavailable," and the call ended.

"What?" I stared at my phone like it was speaking a foreign language. "That's impossible."

"Give me your phone." He reached his hand out to me, his voice friendly, not at all like the troll on the news last night. "Let me check your settings."

I reluctantly handed over my phone while keeping my brow lowered. I wasn't sure what was wrong with my phone, but I knew this was clearly all his fault.

"Yep, just as I figured. You blocked my number." He held his finger next to my contact list. "See, right where it says *Beau*nezer Scrooge. It has my number and it's blocked."

"Wh-what?" My eyes zoomed in, seeing he was, in fact, right. Heat crept into my cheeks. I had no recollection of blocking him, and it made no sense, since I had agreed to work with him. Of course, I would need to talk to him. It must have been subconscious, or an accident. I also had forgotten I had given him that nickname and clearly never planned on him seeing that! "How did that happen?"

"You tell me?" He handed my device back and offered a good-natured shrug.

I kept my eyes on him, hiking both brows defensively. "Are you saying this was my fault?"

"No, that's not what I'm sayin'," he started slowly. "I'm sayin' I did what you wanted me to do, but you were unavailable, so don't be mad at me. I tried to reach out to you."

Feeling this failure deep in my gut, I lowered my eyes. I also didn't know what had gotten into me acting so upset. Beau just brought out the worst in me. I hated how he seemingly had invisible powers over my emotions, just pushing all the buttons that set me off. This wasn't the way I normally treated people, especially my clients. I needed to be better at controlling myself. "I'm sorry," I said in the sincerest voice I could. "I had no idea."

"It's okay." His eye contact was firm, holding me accountable. I held it as long as I could, but he made me uncomfortable. I looked away as he added, "It's not the first time I made everyone on TV mad at me, but now you have to help me fix it."

I gave a shallow nod, knowing it was my mistake that I was out of reach, but I wasn't the one who made him sound like an idiot. The good thing was that I was an expert at cleaning up messes, starting with my own right now. I changed the subject from me and back to him. "You started this dumpster fire. I will agree to fix it this *one* time. If you ever do this again, I'm going to walk away, waving at you while you burn everything down." I didn't give him a chance to say anything because I was so full of his stupid words I couldn't take anymore, so I went on, "News cycles don't last long. They'll have someone else more interesting to talk about by tomorrow."

"So, what do you want me to do?" he asked in an even voice.

I raked my weary eyes over his body, knowing it was time to crank up the electric fence. No more playing around. My voice was low when I asked, "Truthfully?"

His lips stayed apart while he watched me survey him, and his voice was even softer than mine when he said, "Yeah."

"I need you to get a haircut." I breathed out, a little afraid that I might offend him, but I didn't see any way around it. "And some different clothes," I tacked on when I remembered how rig-pigged he had looked during his interview last night. Aside from his brown eyes, I couldn't tell what he even looked like because he had too much unkempt hair. "And maybe shave your beard. And your ears. And buy some stronger soap," I added while staring at his hands, doing my best to infuse an empathetic tone in my voice.

"These are working hands." He held his hands out in front of him, clearly proud of the stains. "Something your generation doesn't seem to understand."

"Beau, I understand how to work hard." My lips twisted up into a sly smile. "I just like to make it look easy." I turned on my heel, heading back toward the door. I was ready to move past this hard conversation, and I knew if I could do this makeover for him, he'd feel better. "We are cleaning up your entire image. I'm going to make it my mission to find you some industrial-grade soap, and if that doesn't work, we'll use acid." I was only half-joking about the acid as I waved him over with urgency. "Come on. We start now."

Six

BEAU

I'd been rockin' this party-in-the-back haircut since I was in grade-school. It truly was the best haircut God could give a man. Short on the sides so you didn't get hair in your face when you're outside sweating. Long in the back, so you had nice coverage from the sun. Could there be anything more genius?

Plus, it looked cool.

I didn't need to waste my breath explaining this. I wasn't prime rib when it came to my looks, and I preferred to ignore them rather than waste time trying to put on swan feathers. Despite my hesitations—and better judgment—here I was at the most expensive spa in town, sitting in the hot seat between Haircut Holly and Clover. "I'm fine if you take a little off my sides." I ran my fingers over my sideburns, trying to distract their attention from my face. I was nervous to see their reactions when they realized all their efforts to pretty me up would be wasted on my ol' country boy face.

"Beau." Clover's words sounded extra choppy when she explained, "We are not asking for your opinion." She patted my shoulder. "I say this with a measure of empathy, but you're going to feel so much better once this is done." Turning to the stylist, she talked over me. "I was thinking of a total buzz. Just chop it all off, so we can see what's underneath and start fresh."

I didn't like how she was speaking 'bout me like I wasn't even here. "Look, Cloverbud," I said, proudly smirking at the new name I had coined for her. "There is no way I'm gonna walk around bald until nature tells me it's time."

Clover's gaze focused on me until I was done talking, but instead of replying, she looked back at Holly and said, "Yep, buzz it all. Beard too. And lots of exfoliation." Her pointed index finger waved over me like she was drawing an air map, with notes on my body. "Scrub behind his ears. That neck dirt collar needs to go too. His nails need something and," with her last breath, she sputtered out, "Moisturizers and sunblock, too."

"I don't need sunblock. My skin's tough as leather," I cut in, but again they ignored me and suddenly, I knew what it felt like to be one of those toy poodles at the groomers.

Holly wrapped a cape around me at the same time she pumped up my chair with her foot pedal, saying, "Relax,

Beau. You are a CEO of a billion-dollar company. It's time you level up and stop acting like you're still the guy behind the shovel. You're going to be a new man when I'm done with you." She handed me a hurricane glass with a pink drink and an umbrella sticking out the top. "Try some of our special dragon fruit white tea."

The only reason I took the stupid drink was because she shoved it in my hand, but I held it out away from me, trying not to catch girly vibes. "I don't drink anythin' pink."

"Just try it," she urged, her red lips curled into a sweet smile. "It'll help with your skin because it has collagen in it."

"I can get my collagen from chicken wings." I snorted, and reluctantly—to get her off my case—I took a tiny sip like I was being asked to drink sour milk. My brows quickly rose as I was pleasantly surprised by the fruity zing that tickled my tongue. Refreshing and hydratin', and it made me want to wiggle my toes.

I wasn't giving into this girly drink, though. Holding it away from my body as though it was about to bite me, I had the perfect view of it. It looked as amazin' as it had tasted. I could see the bubbles spiraling up on the sides, calling to me.

Maybe since I was already holding onto it, I could take another small sip?

So that it would not be so heavy.

Holly was already getting happy with her clippers and paying no attention to what I was doing, so I took another generous sip.

Okay, I might have chugged it when I thought she wasn't lookin', but that pink drink was the best thing I'd tasted all year. There was a reason I didn't trust pink drinks! That stupid sparkle drink relaxed me too much, and I became completely compliant in this makeover, even chuckling happily when I felt the tickle of the clipper on my neck. But my eyes sprang open wide by the tug of the cape unsnapping from my neck as Holly whipped it off, proclaiming, "Tada!"

I jolted, taking in my reflection in the mirror. A young, chiseled face I hadn't ever seen in my life stared back at me. If I had to grade it, I'd call it good as Sunday brisket. "I don't believe it." I touched the side of my cheek, effortlessly gliding over the surface as it was smooth as a baby's backside. "You washed off my tan."

The corners of Holly's lips curled up and her tongue peeked through like it was holding back a chuckle. "You could call it a tan. It's almost the same thing."

My eyes were so wide, you'd think they'd fall out of the sockets, as disbelief washed through me. I walked right up to the mirror and stroked my clean-shaven face as if I was afraid I was in a dream. "How'd you do this?"

"We buzzed it all down and that was underneath. Who knew you were so handsome?" She was still grinnin' at me like a frog in a basket of flies, when she handed me a boutique shopping bag stuffed to the top with tiny boxes. "I put together some skin, hair, and body care products for you."

I took the bag, still holding my face up to the mirror, switching sides, trying to find something that reminded me of my old self.

There wasn't anything.

She had been right.

I was a new man.

A darn good lookin' one too.

"I don't believe it." I looked back at Cloverbud, as she had been silent this whole time while she stood in the background. "Did you know I was going to clean up this good?"

Her eyes rounded like she was holding in a deadly fart, and her words came out quieter than normal. "Trust me. I'm as shocked as you are."

I looked back at the mirror again to make sure my reflection hadn't changed. I couldn't stop rubbing my face. It was so smooth and sleek.

"Well," Cloverbud started, as she moved back toward the door. "We'd better get going if we want to shop for a whole new wardrobe before lunch."

To be honest, after yesterday, I had been doubting my decision to hire Clover. After seeing my transformation—that was all her idea—I thought maybe she knew what she was doing? We had just gotten off on the wrong foot. So, without offering any rebuttal, I strapped on a jovial smile and followed her, cheering, "Let's go, Cloverbud."

Holding up the annoying pointy finger of hers, she snapped, "Don't call me that."

"Too late." I shot finger guns at her, trying to be as annoying as possible because she clearly deserved a little teasing too. "Your name is Clover, and now that you made me look this good, you are definitely my bud."

Her lips remained flat while her hips led the way out of the salon, but I could see she was fighting back a smile.

I was definitely keeping the nickname, and more than likely getting her a T-shirt that said it, too.

Seven

CLOVER

After a full day of shopping with Beau, I drove my financed-up-to-my-neck electric car to pick up my sister from the neighbor's. I let myself in the front door after Lori called me in, and I took one look at Poppy sitting at Lori's picnic style kitchen table, and was instantly tired. "Ah man, Poppy, who gave you gum?" My eyes followed the pink string entangled in her hair. She didn't look at me. It wasn't defiance, though.

I didn't ever remember a time when she had actually looked *at* me.

"Spit it out." I held my hand in front of her mouth, not remotely grossed out. Chewed gum didn't register on the gross scale of things I'd had to do since learning to care for my autistic sister. She pushed her gum out with her tongue right into my palm, and I walked it over to the trashcan in the kitchen, before adding in my best cheerful voice, "So, guess what we get to do?"

No answer, but she heard me. I took the check I had written out to Lori, allocating the last of my savings to her for watching Poppy, and set it on the table. Obviously I thought Poppy was worth the expense, it's just that I didn't really have the money to spend. Now I was paid up for the next two weeks, and if everything went okay with Beau, I would get paid by him right when I needed it the most. I was focused on the positive as I grabbed her hand, and she followed me out the door.

"I found a building. It's right down the street from my work and has a full kitchen and no stairs." I explained as I led the way down Lori's walkway. "I'll have enough money after this month, and I'm going to make an offer." I looked over at her, smiling and wanting so much for her facial expression to match mine, but her face remained indifferent.

We made it to my car, where she got in and buckled herself. I let myself in my car door, still chatting. "After we look at the building, remind me to stop and get peanut butter for your hair." I paused, peering at her in my rearview mirror, imagining she would smile back at me. There was nothing but her spaced-out stare, but even that was beautiful. I always felt she understood me on some level, even if she didn't show it. That is what I told myself anyway, when things got too overwhelming.

I started my car, putting my blinker on, and was waiting to merge into the rush hour traffic, when my phone rang. With one eye on the busy road, I picked up my phone and answered without checking the caller ID. "Hello."

A voice I recognized greeted me. "Cloverbud."

My eyes grew in alarm because there was only one reason he'd call me after work hours. I shut my blinker off and threw my car back in park, ready to give my full attention to this call. "Beau. What have you done?"

"Er, have you been watchin' the news?"

"No, I haven't." Panic seeped into my voice, and I didn't fight it. "What's going on?"

"There was another well explosion just now, but thankfully, everyone is fine. Somehow some video leaked online. Now, there are reporters out in the field. They want to talk to me, but you said not to, so I'm sittin' in my truck, trying to shoo them away. They sure don't get the hint, though."

Two wells in the space of a few days! What kind of insane world have I gotten myself sucked into? My head swelled as I forced a professional tone, "I'm glad everyone is safe." I let out a sigh of relief nobody was hurt, and that Beau had called me. We were making progress with that, at least. "Text me your coordinates and I'll be right there. In the meantime, tell me about this well." I checked my rearview mirror, anxious about Poppy being in the car, but I gunned it anyway, pulling out into the heavy traffic. I was speeding, but I was an excellent driver. This incident was the exact thing Beau did not need right now.

"They won't let you on the site, but if you text me when you get here, I'll direct everyone down to meet ya."

"I'll figure it out. Just tell me what happened. If you did something wrong, I need time to process it."

"We didn't do anythin' wrong. It was one of our wells, but the work had been outsourced to a new contractor. It wasn't our work. However, I have to take responsibility for it."

"Right. But what happened?"

"The landowner didn't want the line trenched into the ground because he was afraid of contamination to his land, so he opted for an above-ground line. People think it's the cleaner option, but you need a converter on it, and those are more dangerous. He wouldn't listen to our warnin', so we did what he wanted. Somethin' must've sparked it. I have no idea what. I'm not a psychic like all these news people think I should be."

"There's nothing else?" I fished in an urgent voice. "You need to tell me everything, Beau, or this won't work. It'll come out eventually, and it's better if we come out with the bad news first.

"That is all I know."

I swerved hard, pulled onto the dirt road that led up to the pumping unit, but I quickly hit the emergency roadblock. "I see your guys. Everything is blocked off. Oh, wait a second. Did you say you are in your truck?"

There was a stony silence before he said, "I'm not driving a scooter to a well site, so you can get that out of your head."

"We will talk more about this later," I said in my best stern voice. "I'm here." I threw my car into park as I grabbed my phone in one hand, and was about to charge out when I caught sight of Poppy in the backseat. Even though she was a full-grown adult, she usually needed some supervision or at least a distraction. I tapped my fingers on the steering wheel as another car parked next to me. It was Susie from channel 5 news! This was not good, and I was wasting time. I don't have a choice.

I texted Beau: "Here. By roadblock. Direct press 2 me."

I turned around and faced Poppy while clearing my throat, warming up my voice for the camera. "Sweetie, I have to go talk to some people. You stay in here, and sit nicely for me. I'll lock the doors, and I promise you'll be fine. I'll be back so fast you won't even notice."

I scrolled through my phone, clearing my throat again, then added, "Ugh, I've got frogs in my throat." I hummed loudly, hearing my voice crack. I finally found a video of funny dogs Poppy liked and handed it to her. "Here, sweetie. Just watch this, and I'll be right back." I cleared my throat one final time, feeling my airway clear. "Finally, I got that frog out," I added, both trying to make Poppy smile, and ease my own nerves, as

I pulled on my door handle. I jogged to the roadblock where a small mob of people waited for me like it was the finish line of the Chicago Marathon.

"Clover." Susie pushed a microphone toward me, not taking time for introductions. "Can you tell us how many animals were injured in the explosion and what Tucker Drilling is doing about it?" Another reporter appeared on my other side, and rudely called out, "Clover, how much will this explosion cost the taxpayers for clean up?" At this point, a whole throng of reporters swarmed me, all pelting me with questions at the same time. I wasn't dismayed, I was born for this. Pulling my shoulders back, I stood tall and grabbed Susie's mic. "Thank you so much for your concern. We are still looking into what might have caused the explosion. I can't comment on that. I can say we are thankful no one was injured. We want to assure you that we will work with top industry environmentalists to get everything cleaned up and back to baseline."

"Clover," Susie went on, "this is the second environmental accident Tucker Drilling has had this month. You would have to agree it appears negligent, and highly alarming, even reckless. Can you tell us about any extra safety precautions Beau is taking to ensure this won't happen a third time?"

"I—" My voice dropped like a hot potato. Poppy was hopping across the roadblock and into the grass like a rabbit, right toward the well fire! "Poppy!" I screamed, my feet propelling me forward. Everyone had been so focused on my interview they missed her passing right through the barricade. "Poppy!" I screamed again and pumped my legs harder. She didn't hear me though, as she was off in her imagination. My heart pounded in an abnormal pattern, notches above healthy pacing. I knew with every fiber of my soul, if I couldn't save her, I would *die* of guilt. "Poppy!" I screamed with every fragment of breath I could squeeze out of my fear-stricken chest.

People say when you are about to die, your life flashes before your eyes, but in this moment, I saw Poppy's life flash before mine. I saw her sitting across from me at the breakfast table, two years old in her unicorn highchair eating cheerios. She had golden pigtails and shining blue eyes that never left mine. I understood back then I was her protector, and I swore to always take care of her.

That was before she regressed.

Next, I saw her the day we found out about her diagnosis. She had lost her words and had been avoiding eye contact for months—if not the better part of a year. Even though we were all heartbroken, mourning all the things she'd never be, she didn't seem to notice as she rocked herself back and forth in her favorite corner.

These sad memories were going to slay me. I pushed them away and ran harder, trying to get to Poppy, screaming like a wild animal was chasing me. The doctors had said she'd never had any vision problems, but she didn't process things the way most people do. She clearly must not see the giant fire she was headed directly towards, or the black smoke rolling out. I couldn't run fast enough, so I screamed again, my voice filled with terror, "Poppy! Stop!"

Then like a country-boy Flash without tights, Beau flew right past me, not slowing until he scooped her up. He flung her over his shoulder, and I held my breath as he returned with her. My eyes cemented on him looking so heroic as he calmly brought my sister back to safety, like it was merely another day at the office for him. It truly was the bravest thing I'd ever seen, and I fought back my sobs so hard it hurt.

All the cameras had shifted to Beau. Even in her high heels, Susie had managed to traipse through the field and catch up to him, jamming her mic right in his face. He ignored her, and I ran up to them, not realizing until now I had given into the tears that poured out of my eyes.

Everything happened so fast, my mind was having a hard time processing it. I slid Poppy off Beau's shoulder and embraced her in a completely selfish hold. Poppy hated to be hugged, or even touched, but I needed to feel her near me to reinforce that she was safe. I fully expected her to wiggle out, or at least struggle, with my squeeze, but she didn't. She slammed her arms around me and held on tight, nestling her head into my neck, and squeezing so hard I struggled to breathe. I didn't care. This was our first real hug, and it brought another sting to my eyes. Having her this close, gave me the reassurance she was going to be okay. My racing pulse slowed to a normal rate, and my heart started to descend out of my throat. Holding back more sobs, and not fully expecting an answer, I leaned in and whispered in her ear, "What were you doing?"

She stared blankly over my shoulder. "I was looking for the frog you lost."

"Wh-what?" I deadpanned, remembering clearly how I had joked about my throat being clogged with a frog. I thought I had been funny, but I had momentarily forgotten Poppy only understood things to be literal. *There was no real frog, but she didn't know that.* Feeling like a failure, again, I saw this was fully my fault.

I was going to have to do better.

As if not wanting to miss her golden chance, Susie pushed that stupid mic at me. But I was done playing their game. PR was one thing. My private family life was another. I ignored her and grabbed Poppy's hand, guiding her toward the car. The media followed, now trying to ask Poppy questions. I couldn't deal with this. My heart was maxed out. I tossed a look over my shoulder, barely regarding them. "Show's over everybody. Go home, or you'll all be reported for trespassing."

I was a master of creating the perception of things looking perfect. Yet, this was too personal for me to care about anything else. I had been careless, and almost lost Poppy. I glanced back at Beau, who locked eyes with me communicating he understood.

"I'm going home," I said, my jaw still quivering. "Just ignore these reporters and I'll handle it in the morning." Without waiting for a reply, I helped Poppy into the front seat and strapped her in. My fingers trembled so hard, I had to retry to click the seat belt three times before it snapped. Hot tears clouded my vision as I clambered back to the driver's seat. I fought back the urge to just gun the engine and tear out of here, but instead, I did the responsible thing and backed out slowly, because the cameras were all still focused on me. It dawned on me it might only be a matter of time before social services would show up, trying to make a case to take Poppy away from me. I pressed one hand against my mouth, stifling the scream I fought so hard not to emit. I flashed my eyes heavenward, and cried out, "I'm sorry, Mom. I failed her."

Eight

CLOVER

I don't remember getting ready for work the following day, but somehow, I managed to pull myself together enough, and dropped Poppy off for another day with Lori, the friendly neighbor. Having hated this routine from day one, I couldn't say I felt any better about it today. I was failing Poppy every day I had to leave her there, but I was doing everything I could to change this situation. I just had to finish my contract with Beau and I'd be able to move forward with her center. With her as my sole motivation, I pushed myself hard, when the only thing I wanted to do was stay in bed all day, and snuggle Poppy while we watch movies and shut out the world.

Since that didn't pay the bills, that was not an option.

Just for today, I allowed myself to keep my phone turned off because I couldn't stomach the news exploiting Poppy.

My heart remained tight, wrapped in a blanket of anxiety as I made it to Beau's office. I felt foolish, and full of guilt that I needed to explain. I forego a traditional hello when I let myself into his office and instead lead with, "It was careless of me to show up to the wellsite like that. I don't know what I was thinking, but from now on I'll handle all emergencies off-site. We'll set up a command center here at your office, where the press will be instructed to meet me."

"That's fine with me." His voice was low, but he did not appear upset as he stared back at me from his leather desk chair.

"But—" I continued in my sullen monotone, as I sank down into the only open chair in the room. "—it seems your on-camera rescue glossed over the explosion, and I haven't had any pushback about that."

He was quiet, and he seemed to be watching me. For once in my life, I didn't feel like working. This was the part of my plan where I needed to help Beau rehearse some media responses, but my brain was fogged up. Everything I did kept pulling it back to Poppy, and oddly something new happened. My eyes had developed a magnetic pull directly to Beau's kind smile. Where once there was a grubby country boy, now stood this . . . this . . . I don't know, but he made my knees like jelly. I forced myself to look away, taking this as the perfect opportunity to bring up something. I shoved my hand into my backpack and pulled out a Gala apple. "This seems weird, but Poppy wanted me to give you this."

His eyes lowered, catching on the apple. He didn't say anything, so I continued, "It doesn't seem like much, but if you knew her, you would understand it's a huge deal. She doesn't talk much, and apples are her absolute favorite food. She doesn't get candy, or any junk food, so this is the sweetest thing she gets during the day, and she looks forward to it all day. She won't even share her apple with me, so I was pretty much stunned when she saved it for you—" My voice trailed off because it sounded stupid to explain something like this to someone who would never understand what it meant for Poppy to do this. "It's sort of a big deal to her." I raised my eyes to meet him as I placed the apple on his desk. "It means she likes you."

His eyes steadied on mine, but he was quiet for a long while before asking, "How is she?"

"She's fine." I don't know, why but I felt like I needed to explain to him, so I tacked on, "she is my sister, and she's autistic. I help care for her." This is the part that always felt weird. I wasn't ashamed of anything, but I constantly grappled with knowing how much was *too* much to tell people. Not because it made me uneasy, but I didn't want to make them uncomfortable. "Both our parents are dead. Nothing tragic. They were wonderful parents but older than average, and now I'm all Poppy has."

He didn't ask me any questions or change the subject, so I continued, "The hardest part is what to do with her during the day. It wasn't bad when she was in school because they would keep her busy, but she graduated last year, and we tried a few work programs, but never found the right fit. Then my mom stayed with her because she was home, but when she passed recently, we ran out of options. I have a neighbor watching her right now, but that is not the right fit as she gets no social interaction with people her age." I don't remember getting up from my chair or starting to pace the room, as it filled my need to fidget, but at this point I was on my second lap and I turned back toward him. "My goal is to open a center for adults where she can go during the day. It's sort of the only reason I took this job working with you because the commission will help with a down payment. If I want to apply for grants, they have strict rules about commercial zoning and all that stuff, and it's been a nightmare . . ." I had said too much, and I guessed by how quiet he was that he probably wasn't even listening. I lowered my eyes and noticed that in addition to the random awkward pacing, I had been picking the skin around my fingernails.

He surprised me by chiming in, "I think that is a great idea."

Despite his approval, it stung a little to look back up at him. I felt exposed. He was a successful entrepreneur, and he would know a lot more about starting a business than I did. For me, it was never about the business side, it was about Poppy, but I still had to find a way to pay the bills. "You do?"

"I do." He nodded slowly like he was giving it proper thought. "Anytime you find somethin' you are passionate about, that makes you the best person to go after it. You are fired up about it." His lips slid into a thoughtful grin when he added, "So, I guess I have her to thank."

The softness in his expression both put me at ease and piqued my interest. "Thank for what?"

"For getting' ya to help me." His eyes found mine in a way that should have been friendly, but combined with his handsome-hunk-makeover, and recent superhero action, it seemed to send an electric spark right to my gut. He tacked on, "It's been a crazy few days, and at first, I wasn't sure what to think about your rescue plan. Well, frankly put, I hated that stupid list of rules, but it's clearly not your first rodeo and I think we might just make it to the finish line."

I opened my mouth to speak, I came up empty. It wasn't the most eloquently stated compliment, but I could tell it was heartfelt. My boss certainly never said that kind of stuff to me. Luckily for me, he didn't notice I was stunned speechless.

He got up from his chair, saying, "Say, I didn't have time to grab any breakfast, and I have a hankering for somethin' fried. Would you want to grab some food with me while we go over your scripts?"

I was starved too, and this weird mood I was in wasn't getting better by sitting here, so I figured we might as well try a change of scenery. "Yeah, I can eat." I stood, stretching my arms high above my head. "I know just the place. It's all organic and they only purchase food from companies who use fair trade, or local farmers." Then I took the lead out of his office, adding, "It'll be good for your image to eat there since it's all eco-friendly." I flashed my phone at him, before stowing it back in my purse. "I'll take a selfie with you to post on social media."

"I said fried. Not tasteless and overpriced toast that you millennials want to invest your 401Ks in."

I sputtered out a laugh, because it was a pretty on-point joke, but I wasn't going to admit that with actual words. Instead, I grinned and motioned to the door and he followed right on my heels. "You keep pointing out my age, like I'm some child. You can't be that much older than I am."

"Eleven years." His eyes slid to the side, catching mine before he tacked on, "I Googled you."

I almost tripped when I heard he had looked me up. I quickly changed the subject, chatting about all the ways you can make avocado toast. I pointed to the corner bistro, his words rolled out unamused, "Stixs and Seeds." He cocked his head and peered down at me. "Are you sure they serve people food? 'Cause that sounds like it's more for a bird?"

"Yes, they serve people food, and it's amazing." My lips turned up into an amused grin. As much as I loved this place for its organic food, I had also wanted to come here to push him out of his comfort zone.

"I ain't no bird." He rubbed his hand over his belly in circles. "I can't live on branches. I need carbs and red meat—preferably somethin' smothered in BBQ sauce—to keep this figure."

"Don't worry." I smoothed over his comment as we passed through the double glass doors into the woodsy décor. It didn't exactly give off a manly comfort food vibe, with the potted trees draped with white Christmas lights. But the birchwood tables were cool, and matched the benches made of long, skinny white logs.

Beau's head took a broad sweep from left to right as he assessed the place, then dropping his voice to a whisper, he said, "It looks like a giant tree house. I present that as evidence to reiterate my point 'bout this being a bird food place."

I stifled a laugh and playfully nudged him with my elbow before whispering, "Too late to turn back now."

"It's never too late to run." He whipped around on his heel, but I was one step ahead of him, and nabbed his hand, pinning him in place. Now I was left holding his hand. *This is strange.* I quickly shook off my hold, but my hand still felt a tingling sensation that was hard to ignore.

A hostess with braided pigtails appeared, cheerily gathered menus for us while chatting about the specials, and ushered us to our seats at a table in the center of the restaurant. We sat, me quietly and ladylike, him with a dramatic sigh and plop. We were way too quiet while we studied our own menus. I couldn't help but keep glancing at him, wishing I could tap into his thoughts. However, the look on his face hinted he might not be that impressed with the menu selection. After an awkward amount of quiet time, Beau spoke with his eyes low on the menu. "I'm gonna tell you something but it's not to spook ya."

"Okaaay." I lingered on the last syllable; my curiosity piqued.

"Just wanna warn ya not to get alarmed if my tooth falls out."

I grimaced at the visual that had given me, turning away slightly as I forced my face into a neutral expression and tried not to show judgment. "Does that usually happen?"

"Not unless I eat somethin' crunchy." He wagged his head reassuringly. "It's a crown. I just glue it right back in as soon as I get to the shop."

I chuckled, not sure if he was being serious or joking, but he never laughed. Instead, he maintained his dead-serious expression. Not wanting him to think I was rude, I slapped my serious expression back on my face and tucked my head down, focusing on picking at my nails. "Glad you warned me."

"Kidding." His laugher rushed out while he struggled to get actual words out, "You believed I would actually glue it back in?"

"I don't know what you would do!" I defended, my face heating up. "I didn't think you'd lie to me."

"It was a joke." He slammed his eyes on mine. "I'm tryin' to get you to lighten up, and it's also payback for making me eat bird food."

"Right." I was smiling now as this whole thing felt so silly. "Except you haven't tried it yet, so you might enjoy —"

"Nope. No, I won't. But I should be able to keep all my teeth." He must have thought he was hilarious since his whole body shook in laughter.

Relief washed over me when our waiter, a college-age male with dreadlocks, strolled over to take our orders, leaving us sitting with two mint waters. I didn't waste any time moving on to phase two of my plan. I shifted right into business mode, "So, thank you for your cooperation with yesterday's task." I pulled out my phone and set it up to record our conversation. "Now, my next task is to write a biography for you which will read like a story. It must be able to connect to people and make them like you. Why don't you start with telling me where you grew up, maybe some of the things you liked as a kid, and how that led to your work now."

"I grew up here in Texas." His lashes fluttered as if he was pulling up a memory. "Like any other country boy, I liked to fish, play football, baseball, and ride motorbikes—" he paused, letting his eyes playfully glare into mine— "gas powered motor bikes. Not electric."

"Right." I held his gaze, but stubbornly didn't laugh at his dig. "Okay, so what brought you to the oil field?"

His thick shoulders raised and lowered. "Just hard work. There ain't any secrets. I wasn't much good at school, except for nap time, and teachers tended to get mad at you for excelling in that subject after kindergarten." He shifted in his seat, adjusted the collar of his shirt, looking uncomfortable but he continued, "I was kind of a loner. Hung out by myself, but I was good at fixin' things and rigging up stuff to work. I didn't want to go to college, so I tried the oil field because something always needs riggin' up there. It seemed like a good match. Nobody made me eat bird food there—"

"—Okay!" I cut off his joke, but my lips betrayed me and curled up as I rushed to ask another question. "Why drilling, and what makes your company special?"

"I never picked drillin'. I think it picked me. I always liked the rush when we first broke ground, and then again, the feelin' I get when we find oil. It's like a treasure hunt." He tilted his head to the side, like he was weighing another thought, and added, "A really long, expensive treasure hunt where mostly stuff breaks down, and you get really dirty, but sometimes you win."

Our waiter returned with our food. My salad looked like another rendition of the same plate of lettuce I ate daily, so I was pleased. Beau, on the other hand stared at his food like it was a road sign he couldn't read.

"What's wrong?" I asked while I spread out my napkin on my lap.

He pushed his fork into his bed of lettuce, lifting it up to see the bottom. "Where is the meat?"

"There is no meat."

"Mine was supposed to come with meat," he insisted. "I ordered the salad under the column that said chicken."

"Oh." I nodded my head knowingly. "It's faux chicken." I pointed to the brown crumbles on the side of his plate. "Right here."

"You mean they don't pluck it?" Beau's eyes slid to the side suspiciously.

"No, *not feather*. Fake. It's fine. Just eat it." I wagged my fork toward his plate. "It tastes just like chicken."

He lightly slapped his palm down on the table. "I get it now." He tossed a look behind his shoulder. "This one of those hidden camera shows?" His lips bent good-naturedly, but the strain in his eyes echoed that he wished it was.

"It's not a TV show. It's chicken."

He raised his brows and exclaimed, "No, it's not chicken! You're telling me fake chicken is a real thing?"

I waved my fork back toward his plate, insisting. "Just try it."

His eyes lowered back to his plate, but the look on his face was still strained. "How come when you fancy people found out hotdogs were mystery meat, you stopped eating them," his tone of voice teasing an argument. "But when you put mysterious meat on a plate of lettuce, you call it "faux" and you're suddenly cultured?"

"I—" I tried to answer his question, but I didn't have an answer. "I don't know what to think about that, but it seems like a valid point." I was done talking about the food and went back to my interview. "So, anyway. That's interesting about the treasure hunt. I would have never described it like that, but you made it sound appealing." Pursing my lips, I thought about the best way to phrase my next question, before continuing, "I've been wondering why since you run a successful company and have a lot going on with running it," I motioned to him across the table. "Why do you still feel the need to work with the guys in the field?"

His brow dropped, giving him an expression of confusion. "Why would I not? I can't ask my guys to do the grunt work if I'm not willin' to do it too."

"Right." I nodded, showing I heard, but I needed clarity. "It's just not typical for a CEO."

"A business runs the best when the guy in charge shows up." He wagged his head back and forth, like he couldn't understand why I would think it was odd. "I find the best way to motivate your boys is to work next to them." He shrugged his shoulders and stared blankly back at me.

I was about to call it good and stop recording, but he surprised me by picking up our conversation again. "I know you think drilling oil is dirty, and the root cause of all things killing this planet. All you hippies do, but I see it differently. I'm helping people and savin' lives."

I slid to the edge of my seat, letting his words ring in my ears for a minute before I responded. "How so?"

"Look at the products oil makes. Try to live a day without oil, and you can't. There isn't a substitute on the planet as efficient and versatile as oil. And it's cost-effective. The fact we can drill it out of our own soil is the biggest benefit of all because it gives high-paying jobs back to our communities."

"High paying jobs, at what cost?" I wasn't convinced. In fact, I was insulted. So much so, my heart ramped up a notch. "There're lots of products available from our own soil that can do the same things oil can, but they also don't pollute the planet. I think your statement is very close-minded of you."

He squared his jaw while he replied in an even tone. "I'm realistic."

My tongue felt tacky, and I had to open my mouth wider to articulate my words. "No. You say you can't live without oil like it's a blanket statement, but you haven't even tried."

His head tilted toward me in a curt nod. "Have you?"

"Not specifically." My lips tightened, and my eyes hovered over his as the burn of annoyance budded in my chest. I selected my words carefully. "I'm open-minded enough to at least consider it."

"Consider it?" One brow arched above the other, and his voice lowered into his gruff gravelly one. "I dare you."

I cringed, feeling personally attacked. "Dare me to do what?"

"Put action behind your words." He motioned to me with his fork. "Spend twenty-four hours without using any products made with oil."

"Then what?" I asked flatly. I didn't see where he was going with this stupid dare that was so easy a fly could do it.

"I don't know. How 'bout bragging rights. If you can do it, I'll toss another ten grand into your contract."

My jaw dropped so low it must have looked broken. I had no clue why this was so important to him. I also didn't understand why he was trying so hard to convince me. "Ah, for real?"

"For real." He wagged his index finger in the air in a way that was so annoying, it made me want to bite it. "Just try. You can test your hypothesis to see if you can do it, or not."

I narrowed my eyes, letting my tongue swipe the front of my teeth as if it alone was responsible for mustering up my courage. I jutted my jaw and bravely asked, "When do I start?"

"I reckon since you are sittin' on logs cut with gas-powered chain saws, and you're in an air-conditioned building fueled by natural gas, unless you wanna to give up now, I'd wait until after dinner. Maybe just so you can finish the day in the comfort of your air conditioning. You know, I wouldn't want to shock you by makin' you too uncomfortable."

I didn't flinch this time. "Deal."

"Just like that?" His gaze was skeptical when he added, "Don't you wanna to ask any questions, or plan this out a little better?"

"Nope." I offered him my I-couldn't-care-less-about-this shrug. "How hard can it be?"

"For starters, how do you plan on gettin' home?" He tilted his head, looking at me a little sideways. It was a cocky expression I hadn't seen before, and I hated it.

"Ah, I have an electric car," I spit back like I had the ace card.

"Right. And you do know charging stations get power from the grid." When I didn't reply, he added, "So the grid is fueled by coal, natural gas and all the dirty stuff you hate."

I fought the urge to put my hand on my hip. "I charged it at home."

"And your home is hooked up to the grid which means—not green."

I flicked my bottom lip against my top teeth to enunciate, "Fine." After I glared at him for an appropriate amount of time, I tacked on, "I'll walk."

"You can walk home but can't use any power or lights when you get there."

I crossed my arms over my chest, and slumped way down in my chair. I knew what he was doing. Did he think I wasn't aware of all the ungreen products in our daily lives? *I was the Queen of Green!* "I'll go camping."

"Well, forget about bringin' a cooler, or a tent, because those are most likely made from oil products."

"I have an organic cotton pillow and comforter. That's all I need." My words were measured and harsh. I was ending this conversation now.

"No shampoo bottles, or plastics, anything charged on the grid, no—"

"I get it!" I cut him off, straightening my spine. I was so wholly agitated I couldn't contain my composure any longer. "Stop trying to be a know-it-all rig pig because I know what you are trying to do. You're trying to teach me a lesson, but you'll be surprised because I'll be able to do this. I'll walk home, and just so I don't accidentally flip a light switch or unintentionally step into air conditioning, I'll grab my stuff and go to the park to camp. It's only one night. I'll be fine.

Actually, I'll be better than fine. It'll be so refreshing, I'll add years to my life!"

His eyes traced my face, but his lips never cracked a smile as they maintained a serious expression. "Me, a know-it-all-rig pig?" A snort leaked before he went off, "You're a know-it-all-hippie with an ugly nose antenna! I bet you can't tell me why this is so important to you."

Nose antenna! It's called self-expression! Now I was so white hot mad at him I didn't think he even deserved a chance for me to explain this to him. "Because—" I started but then stopped so I could swallow and wash some of my anger down. I tried again, my words laced with spit, "It's important we start cleaning up our environment, and every little bit matters. I'll show you it's easier than you think." I pushed my salad forward as I was done talking. I was so completely aggravated now, that I shot to my feet and declared, "I'm ready to go."

"See, I knew you didn't like the food—" He stood, pulled out his wallet, and dropped a hundred-dollar bill on the table. "Looks like someone is already being a sore loser." His voice was taunting, but he didn't fall behind as I strode toward the door.

Gritting my teeth, I bit out, "I never lose."

He elbowed me with a nudge that failed to be friendly. "First time for everything, Cloverbud."

I inclined my chin in the air, proclaiming my plans, "Just so you know I won't be cheating, I'll be camping at Central Meadows Park. You're welcome to come spy on me to ensure I'm not accidentally siphoning off someone's grid."

He chuckled in an octave so low and dark it made Ebenezer Scrooge sound like Tinkerbell. We passed through the restaurant doors, stepping onto the sidewalk and right into the wind. A smile crossed his lips. "You have fun because it's supposed to storm tonight."

"I will!" I huffed before speeding off, leaving him to eat my trail of attitude. I was done with him. Thanks to my makeover, Beau Tucker was no longer a greasy, greedy rig pig anymore. He was a hunky and cocky jerk! Which made it even more important for me to win.

Nine

CLOVER

Gray clouds rolled in, but I didn't give them a second look as I powerwalked the path in the park, scouting for the perfect spot to spend the night. It only took me a little over an hour to trudge the five miles out here. I could have found a closer park, but the one nearest my apartment was right in the center of town and had a lot of noisy traffic. This park was right on the edge of the lake with regular campsites that were a peaceful place to spend the night under the stars.

Walking had felt good; it helped me to blow off some of my pent-up frustrations with Beau. I couldn't believe he was being such a jerk over this. He obviously knew my entire business was founded on creating a greener planet, and since all I did was work, that meant my entire identity was wrapped in this mission. I mean, my business card says, "The Green Queen." That wasn't just a slogan, *it was my life!*

It was frustrating because he had complied with all the tasks, I had asked of him, and I had started to think maybe he did want to change. Now, I was sure all the progress we made was fake and he did it to save face. Which only infuriated me more. There are lots of fake people in the world, but I had started to think he was sincere.

Or maybe I had started to like him—

Whoa! Where did that come from?

I startled and checked around me, expecting someone to be standing there inserting random terrible ideas into my head.

I mean, *come on*!

I swept my hair to the side, pulling it over my shoulder. Clearly, I was overtired. This week had been far too stressful. A night alone, to recharge was exactly what I needed. This was going to be fun. Stopping in front of a giant tree, I decided this looked like a nice place to rest my back against, and I dropped my backpack and sat down next to it.

While I unzipped my bag, and dug through its overstuffed contents, I mused about how easy and great this was going to be. I had brought books to read, but— Looking around, I realized even though there was a lamp post not too far away, it wasn't bright enough for me to be able to read actual paper pages with tiny print.

Clearing *that* idea from my head, I dug back into my bag, pulling out a deck of cards. "Ah," I sighed to myself satisfactorily. "Nothing like a good old fashion game of Solitaire."

I shuffled the deck three times, and started to deal my cards, but then I noticed the wind had gotten a little strong, and my cards weren't staying in a line.

"Okay," I said out loud. "New plan. I'm going to have a snack"—I pulled out my bag of dried bananas and a notebook— "and plan Poppy's center." I took my pen out and wrote:

Things I have done:

1.Found a building.

2.Applied for funding.

3.Applied for grants.

4.Applied for a business license.

Things I need to do:

1.Get approved for my loan.

2.Ask Beau if he ate his apple—

"Ah!" My body jolted, and I dropped my book like I had found a spider on my page. *Why would I write that?* I asked out loud, then slammed my book shut, and stuffed it back into my backpack like I was trying to conceal crime scene evidence.

Relax, I breathed.

I wrote it, because Poppy *gave* it to him, and I was thinking about *Poppy*.

Because I WASN'T thinking about Beau!

Because why would I be thinking about Beau?

Because Poppy gave him an apple because Beau rescued her.

Yeah, my eyes dropped to the side as I recalled the memory. He looked HOT when he did that.

What!

I literally smacked the side of my face, trying to get the image of Beau out of my head. *Why he is affecting me like this?*

I mean, I was mad at him, clearly there was no way I could like him.

The evidence was obvious as I was camped out in the park tonight, by myself. I had bribed Charlotte to sleep at my apartment—that was much cozier and warmer than out here—to watch Poppy. I would never do that if I wasn't furious with him.

It was like the wind read my thoughts and decided to tease me, opening up with a hard gust of wind, sending chills all through my body. I hugged my jacket tighter.

"Brr," I hummed to myself. It had cooled off quite a bit now, and something wet hit my cheek.

"It has to be almost morning." I checked my watch, feeling my heart fall. I had only been here fifteen minutes. I felt another drop of water, smacking my arm this time. "I don't know if I want to stay the whole night." I looked out into the black night—okay, I'll admit a little creepy dark night—hoping to see something to distract me.

"Nope." I popped the p, as I continued to talk to myself, hoping the noise of chatter would calm the quibbles starting to bubble in my gut. "Nobody's here."

Now the regular patter of rain was tapping down on me, wetness started to penetrate my clothes. I scooted on my bottom, angling my body away from the wind as much as I could to try to avoid the rain, but as many times as I shifted, it made no difference. The wind whirled in all directions, throwing the rain in huge waves slamming against me. I haughtily pulled my blanket out of my backpack, draping it over me for protection, but moments later, it was soaked all the way through.

My eyes landed on my backpack. It was an old one I had used in high school, and it wasn't getting wet at all. The raindrops were rolling right off it. I ran my fingers along the side, brushed off a few drops that had beaded up. *My backpack was made from PVC and waterproof!* Normally I would be appalled to have such a possession but tonight it was my lifesaver. I quickly zipped it back up, and stacked it on top of my head, shielding me from the rain. It helped but it didn't stop the shivers dotting along my spine, as I was already soaked.

This was absurd!

I had become one of those ridiculous people who would do anything for money. I wasn't compromising my values or anything terrible like that. If anything, I was sticking to them, as I was out here, shivering away, doing this to defend my values as well as earn some extra money to pad my savings account. Money that would make it easier for me to continue to care for Poppy until I got her center up and running. Money that would make my life easier in the short term. *Had I taken this whole thing too far?* It didn't seem fair because I hadn't planned on it storming this badly. It wasn't worth getting sick over. If I got sick, then I clearly couldn't work or take care of Poppy which would set me way back on my goal. It wasn't worth a stupid bet, and I tapped my jacket pocket, out of habit, trying to find my phone to call for a ride, but I remembered I had purposely left my phone at home.

My scared-blank-stare froze my face.

No phone was not good.

Home was too far to walk, especially in this rain. Tears budded as I tried to think of any local businesses near the park where I could run to take shelter, but everything was so far away. There wasn't anything nearby as the park was on the outskirts of town. Without a phone, there wasn't anyone I could call.

Lightning flashed overhead, splitting the sky into two halves. It was so brilliant of a light; it left me frozen until the whip crack sound of the thunder so deafening it shook the whole ground, made my butt tingle. I pulled my legs into me, curling up into a ball, and cried, "I want to go home!"

Ten

BEAU

I unpacked my takeout onto a TV tray in my living room, the same thing I did every night—add in a beer or Coke and rerun of somethin' stupid. I kicked back in my favorite recliner, and I was happy as a pig in sunshine. I peeled back the wrapper on my spicy pulled-pork sandwich, removed a nice meaty chunk, and tossed it to Bandit, who snatched it right up.

Bandit was my beagle—mixed with somethin' ugly—that I picked up outta the ditch a few years back. If I had my druthers, I'd never get a dog, let alone a mangy mutt like him, but now that I had him, we were two peas in a pod. He only did one annoying thing— he licked my feet while I ate.

There undoubtedly was something wrong with him. If I didn't find it against my religion, I would have given him a big ol' kick in the head, but I was never the type of man who could hurt an animal. Instead, I took him to the vet to see if he had some weird disease, but the doc said he was normal. Then I thought it had to be the soap I used, so I switched to a new kind. That didn't stop him. To date, I have tried many different types of soap, only to conclude it doesn't matter.

I finished my dinner, relishing every delectable and juicy, barbecue-slathered bite until I was so full, I had forgotten all about that stupid bird lunch. Tonight, the wind was blowin' up a storm. I cranked the gas on my fireplace, my lips bending upward at how slick that worked. Oddly, it made me think of Cloverbud being defensive in her use of gas earlier. A rush of laughter fell from my mouth as I thought about her having that good ol' dying duck fit over the mere suggestion she couldn't live without oil. Like I really cared if she used oil or not? I was only tryin' to get a rise out of her.

And it worked.

I scratched the top of Bandit's head and muttered, "I don't know what I'd do with a hippie anyway."

My hand froze mid-scratch.

Did I just say *that*?

Why would I say *THAT*?

Pfft. I must be worn slap out. I clicked the remote on the TV to turn it off and let my eyes shut, willing myself to fall asleep in my chair—the same place I slept every night because it was cozier than sleeping in a king bed by myself.

Sometime after midnight, I awoke to thunder cracking that sounded like it was right in my living room. It was so loud,

I sat up straight and was fixin' to run for my rifle. A flash of lightning split the sky right outside my window. My ears perked up as I listened to the rain clap on my roof. It was a real frog sampler.

I was 'bout to roll over to sleep, but Bandit crawled up next to me, his whole body shaking in fright. I wrapped my arms around him, tucking him in, but it didn't stop the shuddering. I'm not sure why, but it made my mind turn back to Cloverbud stuck out in the rainstorm without even so much as a tent to cover her head. Part of me wanted to snicker, but my good side slapped that part, and said *go get her*.

As much as she got my goose, I could never let a lady get struck by lightning.

Only one problem.

All my two-seater vehicles were on lockdown.

I wasn't sure what the owner's manual said about ridin' these scooter death traps in a rainstorm. I reckoned it wasn't good, but I wouldn't pretend I hadn't done stupider.

One of the bonuses I learned was, you could ride two-wheelers up on the curb, through people's yards, and you didn't have to follow general traffic guidelines. I made like spaghetti and wove through traffic, rain pourin' down until I made it to the park. I was off-roading, slidin' in the mud like a wet pig as I pulled up on her, flashing my single headlight. She wasn't hard to spot, sitting underneath a big ol' tree with a dinky backpack on her head.

Just as I reckoned.

She didn't have the sense God gave a goose.

"What're ya doing, trying to get all electrocuted?" I yelled over the wind as I gestured to the tree above her head, like she was sending up a lightning rod.

Her eyes popped wide, like they were already fried, and she sprang to her feet, bolting directly at me. I thought she was gonna shout at me the way she was running so frantically, but instead, she flew right to me and smacked a wet slobbering rainstorm kiss right on my cheek.

That was different.

Even though the rain quickly washed it away, it tickled where her lips had touched.

I froze, waiting for her to do something.

She covered her face with her hand like she was as surprised as I was, and backed away from me slowly. She was visibly trembling and hugging herself. "Ah, sorry. I was relieved to see someone."

"You'd better come back before you get imprinted into the ground."

Her pouty lip pushed out as if she was gonna argue, but instead she hustled to the back of the scooter and climbed on. As I took off back in the direction I had come, the wind howled even more, making the rain swirl all around us. I couldn't see the broad side of a building. I had to scream at the top of my lungs. "Why didn't you call for a ride?"

"I don't have my phone because you said I can't use anything that charged on the grid."

I gritted my teeth and shook my head. "You are one stubborn hen."

Nothing from her.

"Where do you live?" I hollered back at her.

"Bloomgrass Village."

"Way over there? We'll never make it in these winds," I yelled, but I doubted she heard anything. I decided to drive her back to my place. She didn't pitch a fit when I pulled my scooter into my garage. I didn't think I had to explain to her what was going on, so all I said was, "My place was closer. You can wait it out here, or call a cab."

"I don't think any cabs are out in this storm." She eased off my scooter like she was still a little spooked. Her teeth were chattering so loud they reminded me of a pair of those wind-up ones. I had to turn my head because her clothes were so drenched, I swore I could see her religion. "Wow." She scanned the garage bay next to us, pausing on each one of my arcade machines. "You have a whole game room in here."

"I'm a collector." I grinned, tacking on, "It's a hobby. I like to keep busy, and I have loved arcade games since I was a little kid."

"You have Pac-Man." Her gaze froze on my machine.

"Not just Pac-Man." I moved toward the machine and placed a hand lovingly on it. "A 1980, first-edition in mint condition. I drove all the way to Montana to get it. She was hurt really badly when I brought her home, but I got her workin' again."

"So, you restore them?"

"It's better than letting them go into a landfill." Both my brows raised defensively, thinking she thought this was a childish hobby. "These games are a part of our history, plus they are fun to play."

She held her hand up gently, clearing the air of any tension. "I didn't mean to offend you. I was actually impressed. You upcycle them. That's very green of you."

There was something funny 'bout looking at her next to my machine. I had a hard time not staring at her, so I quickly turned to the machine, creating a distraction. "I don't know what color it is, but I call it, you're gonna lose." I flipped the switch, firing up the machine. Her eyes glittered back at it when the lights flicked on, and I strapped on a grin and said, "I challenge you to a match."

"A match, oh, um." Her eye lashes fluttered a few times. "You mean you want me to play?"

"Yeah, unless you're scared."

"No." The tips of her lips curled. "I can totally win at Pac-Man" She stepped forward, taking her place in front of the joystick, and I pressed the start button. I'd played this game so many hours, I could play it with one eye—while I kept the other on her. It didn't take her long to replace the straight-brow expression she normally wore with a new expression with uplifted brows which brightened her whole face.

Even though she died right away, she laughed and eagerly accepted another turn. When she died the second time, her smile broadened, and laughter funneled out joyfully. "Okay, maybe I exaggerated, and I can't win."

"Ah." I switched the machine off, and backed away, "It's not about winning anyway." I tossed a shoulder up, adding, "Something to do." I suddenly remembered it was way past midnight, and she was standing in the middle of my garage, look like a wet hen, and I returned to my manners. "Let's get you inside, so you can warm up." I walked ahead, and she was right on my heels as I went through the door.

"You better go sit by the fire." I motioned to my favorite chair with the fire still roaring next to it. "I can grab you a dry t-shirt." I left to go down the hall to the laundry room and grabbed one of my shirts from the dryer. It had gotten a little wrinkled from sitting there for a few days, but I shook it. It didn't really help the wrinkles but I figured it had to be better than what she had.

When I returned, she was sitting on the fireplace hearth, leaving the chair open. I wanted to tell her how stupid she was for testing that storm, but I figured she already had to know. So instead, I looked at her and grinned, pretending she didn't get my goose. "I don't have any groceries or anythin' because

I don't cook, or ever have company over, but I can get you something to drink."

"It's okay." She lowered her eyes. "I'm fine sitting here."

I set the shirt down next to her and peered out the window, noticing the wind hadn't let up at all, if anything it was only hollerin' louder. "It's a good thing we got back when we did. It's ugly out."

Her eyes steadied on the fire, as if she was avoiding looking at me.

"I don't mean to be harsh, but is there a reason you had to be so stubborn about this oil thing?" I asked with a light-hearted chuckle. "It isn't a good reason to catch your death out there."

Although she kept her gaze at the fire, I caught a glistening off her eyes. She spoke in a softer voice, like she was reading a fairy tale. "It seems silly, and I don't expect you to understand, but it's something I do for Poppy. There's evidence autism is caused by environmental factors and it's one thing I have control over."

I hiked a brow. "Trying to get killed?"

Her face turned down, signaling she was withdrawing from the conversation, but she did eventually add, "I don't think there is anything wrong with having a cleaner planet."

I shrugged, kinda seeing her point. "I mean, I agree there isn't any harm in cleaning up the place before we leave, but I also don't think modern civilization would be better off without oil. Maybe someday we will get to that point, but you gotta admit, it would have been a lot cooler if I'd rescued you in my pickup truck, or shoot, one of my sports cars."

The corners of her mouth bent up a tiny bit. "I guess that would have been a lot nicer, but I appreciate you showed up at all." With eyes fixed on her fingernails. She picked on them like it was an Olympic sport. "Thank you."

Her words floated out and hung in the air, and just to get a rise out of her, I teased, "You already said thank you when you kissed me."

Her cheeks instantly blushed. "Clarification." She held up her arguing finger. "I kissed your cheek. Not the same as kissing you."

Maybe I liked poking the bear? I decided to poke a little more. "Can you stop shredding your nails before you bleed out all over my floor? One near-death experience for the night is enough for me."

She laughed. Not one of those polite little giggles, but a genuine full belly laugh, and her gaze rose and attached to mine.

I wasn't sure what to think about that.

I wasn't an expert in females, but those were flirtin' eyes.

It wasn't the first time I had a woman look at me like that, but it was the first time I saw that expression from Clover-bud.

Those were the kind of looks that got me into trouble.

I pulled at the collar on my t-shirt as the temperature in the room seemed to heat up a few degrees.

Then she did it.

The look away, acting all cute. Like she didn't know what she was doing.

She was as pretty as a peach sitting there next to the fire. Her whole profile was lit up in a glow like she was something extraterrestrial. An angel, perhaps? Even though none of the angels I ever read up on had nose rings. I reckoned it could serve as a modern version of a halo.

"I think you were a little bit right."

"Ah," I deadpanned even though I liked the sound of that phrase, the softness etched in her words put my heart on alert.

"About the oil thing," she went on. "I took everything so personally because I've worked for a decade trying to get companies to be greener, and it's been a long road. I hated to hear that maybe it was for nothing."

"Well, it's not for nothin'. But these sorts of things take time." I thought we were done talking because it was getting awfully late. My guess was she was delirious, but she took the conversation in a different direction—one that slapped the sweat right on my back.

"Do you ever think about love, Beau?"

My breath jammed in my chest, and I made one of those gruntin' swallows. My voice was rendered useless, so I stretched my neck, trying to pull some oxygen in. When that didn't work, I twisted the other way like I was practicing for an exorcism.

She was batting her lashes like a toad in a hailstorm.

Shoot.

I was sugar in her hand.

I didn't have the slightest clue how that happened.

"Ah, nope, can't, never could, and won't think about love," I rattled out so many negative words, my old English teacher's head would have exploded. I quickly crossed to the window, closing the curtains tight. "I reckon this storm is gonna blow all night. We might as well settle in. I gotta be on site by sunrise, so I need a few hours of sleep." I announced as I focused on not looking at her. "The washroom is right down the hall. You really should put on that dry shirt. There's a guest room right there on the left and you're sure welcome to sleep in it."

I didn't glance back before heading upstairs because I didn't want any trouble.

At least not *tonight*.

I wasn't afraid of trouble. I actually rather liked it. However, I was a country boy, and my mama taught me how to treat a lady, and do things properly. Any trouble I get into is always done properly.

Eleven

CLOVER

Sometime in the middle of the night, I dozed off and was awakened the next morning by the sound of chirping outside the window. And a yellow Post-it note on my forehead. "I got a ride to work. You can take my scooter." I squinted through one eye, rereading it as my confusion mounted. I recognized Beau's house.

And I remembered last night!

My heart motored fast as the panic seeped all the way up to my throat, irritating it enough to make me feel like throwing up. I wasn't sure what was more humiliating. Beau pulling me out of the storm on his electric scooter, or the way I tried flirting with him afterward.

Who was I kidding?

I smacked my forehead, feeling the shame claw its way further up in my throat. It was definitely my ill-advised attempt at flirting. When he showed up in the middle of that storm with a storm of his own in his eyes, I felt like I was struck by a lightning bolt. Something hit me right in the chest and didn't stop until it implanted in the vicinity of my heart. It took on a life of its own, swelling each time I gazed into his dreamy eyes, colored just like my favorite 80% dark chocolate.

I had never had an experience like that before.

Once I gave into my thoughts, I couldn't find an excuse to push them away. He wasn't the Beau I had thought he was. As I unpacked this idea even more, I made a list on my fingers.

This Beau was funny.

This Beau was kind.

This Beau was handsome.

Sure, he was a rig pig, but he was a rig pig with heart.

Not only did he selflessly charge out to save Poppy, but last night he was my own just-in-time hero, and his actions opened my heart in a way that it hadn't been in a long time—if ever. It wasn't overdone, but just sweet enough. More than that, I didn't want to fight these feelings. I'd been single so long, and there wasn't anything wrong with having a little innocent crush.

Sure, we were working together, but that would end soon, and then what? Maybe this was fate? I tucked the Post-it note in my pocket and got up. Destination: garage. Since I had already lost the bet, I eagerly strapped on a helmet, straddled on Beau's scooter, and headed toward my apartment to clean up.

I arrived home and found Charlotte sitting at the table, sipping coffee. "Hey," I half-whispered, unsure whether Poppy was still sleeping. "How'd it go last night?"

Her eyes met mine, but she didn't smile. My heart ticked up a notch as I lowered myself to the chair next to her, and kept my voice low while I asked, "What happened?"

Wagging her head back and forth, she kept her lips sealed. I pressed my hand on her arm. "Just tell me. Nothing will surprise me."

"It was fine." She ran a hand through her dark hair, smoothing out the soft waves. "I could just tell she would much rather have had you here. She seemed so out of sorts."

"How so?" I leaned forward, my trepidation growing.

"Nothing in particular." She paused after each word, her sentence seeming to take forever. "She's a sweet girl, but let's say I have a huge new appreciation for what you do."

My blood pressure slowed as I realized nothing major happened. "Did she eat?"

"She had her apple, but wasn't interested in any dinner. I tried to get her to munch on some of that paleo stew you had in the fridge for her, but I think her stomach was bothering her."

"Ah, yeah." I sighed, feeling bad I hadn't been there for her. "I noticed that when I picked her up from the neighbors. She seemed a little bloated."

"I'm sure it was nothing." Charlotte waved her hand dismissively.

"Thank you so much for helping me." I felt bad I only had verbal appreciation to offer her.

"Don't mention it." She stood slowly and pushed her chair back close to the table while looking at me. "How'd the bet go? I was worried about you once the thunder started. Did you win the money?"

"No." I had mostly forgotten about the stupid bet as I was now more concerned about how I had embarrassed myself by flirting so badly. "I gave up because of the rain. Beau showed up and rescued me."

"Oh." Her eyes stayed straight, but it felt like she was fighting back asking more questions. "Well, I'm glad you're safe."

"Yeah, me too."

"I'm going to head home, and spend my Saturday binge watching my new show. Call me if you need anything."

"I will." I nodded. *Why was she looking at me like I was about to crack?* I was totally fine and completely used to my new life and *all* these extra responsibilities. Not sure why my eyes would be stinging right now. I was sure they were irritated from the weather change. Trying my best to blink the annoyance away, I had one more favor to ask. "Say, since you offered, there's this environmental fundraiser tomorrow night. I might need to go to—"

"Oh sure. Of course," she said matter-of-factly. "I can watch her again."

I froze. I wasn't expecting to get emotional about something so simple. It was a normal thing to need childcare, only I didn't have a child. I had an adult sister with a disability. I had no idea what I was doing. I never took a class in high school—or even college—that prepared me for this experience.

I was facing Charlotte, but all I saw was my mom's face, and how I missed her so much. Not just because she took care of Poppy, but because she had been my best friend. As much as I missed her, I was relieved she wasn't actually here, because I wouldn't have been able to look her in the eye and tell her how badly I was messing up. A heaviness I could only describe as the weight of failure filled my chest. "I'm sorry to ask again," I squeaked out. "I'm trying hard to get Beau's case finished so I can get paid and—"

Reaching a hand to mine, she gently squeezed and said, "You don't have to explain. It's okay. You are doing amazingly and I'm happy to help."

I felt foolish for feeling like I was going to cry over something so stupid as having to ask for a favor. She repeated,

"You're doing amazingly." She smiled sweetly. "Better than amazing."

Blinking back my guilt, I swallowed, and whispered, "I'm trying."

"I know." She released her hand from mine, and added, "Everything's going to be fine. It takes time." She took another step closer to the door, slower this time, her eyes not leaving my face. "Text me when you know what time you need me."

"Thank you." I tried to say it out loud, I only managed to mouth the words. Thankfully, Charlotte understood, and she continued to smile warmly before leaving me to figure this out on my own.

Things were so different now. It was easier when I was only Poppy's fun sister. Now I had all these decisions to make, and no one had given me the instruction manual. Worse yet, I didn't have the time I needed to consider things as thoroughly as I would have hoped. One decision after another was thrown at me, and things only sped up. It was exhausting. I didn't think I ever appreciated my mom more than I did at this moment, and it felt too late.

I spent the day with Poppy, doing all the things she loved, from feeding the ducks in the creek behind our apartment, to swinging for hours on the tire swing on the tree at the park. If only I could do that with her every day. It wasn't a perfect day, but we made some memories and refueled my soul.

Now, I was waiting for Beau in a downtown parking lot, ready to start phase three of his makeover. I checked my phone for a message, noting the time. I had convinced him to appear with me at the Green Charities Fundraising Gala, and he was running more than fashionably late.

Drumming my fingers on my leg, I tapped out a tune that had gotten stuck in my head as I watched other couples walk past me on their way inside. Everyone was dressed in formal wear, as this was the trendiest who's-who event of the year. I had rented a couture gown from an online dress rental place. I hadn't tried it before, but I was glad I did. I felt like Princess Aurora, letting my hair flow in loose curls down my back in this gown that was fit for a ball.

Anybody who was anybody would be here tonight to be seen supporting their favorite charity. This would be an essential step to improving Beau's image, but it was only going to work if he showed up on time.

Giving up, I pulled out my phone again and tapped his name, pressing send. His phone rang, going right to voicemail. I was about to leave a message when a gruff voice bellowed from behind me. "Sorry, I didn't recognize you in that dress. I was waiting inside."

"What?" I spun around. The sun was starting to crest at that awkward angle that made everything hard to see. The man before me appeared to be glowing. Taking a step closer to him, I halted fast, my phone dropped to my side. My legs grew weak, and a spark shot through my body.

This man in front of me was no Beau.

He sounded like Beau.

He was as tall as Beau.

But this man was straight out of a fairy tale prince casting call!

It didn't help that the sun was working as his wingman, and his skin seemed to literally sparkle as if it was a sign from my fairy Godmother that he was a secret prince. He had donned a debonair black tux, complimenting his deep tan, and it all seemed to highlight his natural height. All that darkness contrasted with the bright white of his eyes, made those a focal point, which sucked me right in with their dreamy warmth.

I had been the mastermind behind his initial makeover, but something else had happened since then. He'd developed some swagger that drew me toward him. I fought it by avoiding direct eye contact, but not before I took control of my mouth and sputtered out, "Graw! You look—"

"I know you're mad," he blurted out, thankfully speaking over my word vomit. "I'm sorry. I was here, though. I'm not late. I didn't see you. Actually, I mean, I saw you standing here, but I didn't recognize you. You look different. I expected you to look, you know. Like you."

That shouldn't have made any sense, but it totally made all the sense in the world because it was exactly how I was feeling! If I had to admit it, I had seen this handsome man walk past me earlier, but I had absolutely not thought for even a tiny second, that it was Beau! "It's fine." I tugged at my ear, pretending to adjust my earring while trying to sound casual. "I think I saw you, but didn't recognize you either."

He clapped his hands in front of him like he was ready to start a tour. "So, what's the plan?"

"Ah, yes." I held up my phone again, tapping on my notes. "I made a list of the booths we need to visit. I want you to try to hang out in front of each booth for a good ten minutes to make it appear that you are interested. Ask them as many questions as you can, and get names. Then at the end of the night, I want you to pick one charity for a donation, and we will try to get photos with all of them. I'll post and tag everyone on social media tomorrow."

His eyes narrowed, like he had seen something disgusting. His bottom lip rolled under his top as though holding back his words.

When he didn't release his thoughts, I asked, "What is it?"

"Nothing."

"No, it's something." I parked my hand on my hip, my patience growing slim. I'd always been a straight shooter and didn't like playing word games. "If you have a problem with something, let me know. I can take a booth or two off the list if you really can't stomach them."

"It's not the booths." His lashes raised way up, and he studied the sky. "It's just, I thought we came to have fun."

"Fun?" I didn't know why I sounded like a disapproving-mean-old granny. I blamed it on my surprise.

"Yeah, you know, like doin' something for a purpose that doesn't gain you something productive." He motioned to the building where two couples were standing in front, laughing cheerily. "But I guess if your idea is better, then I'll stick to your plan." He reached his hand forward. "Here, let me look at your list."

Now I felt foolish. I came here with a plan to finish my list in an efficient manner. Charlotte was watching Poppy, and I hated having to rely on her for help, but this was an important step in Beau's image makeover. I honestly hadn't thought of staying around to enjoy myself. I never did that, but maybe?

I could be fun!

That sounded fun!

I quickly texted Charlotte, letting her know it would be another late night. Guilt rushed into my brain, nagging me that Poppy needed me. I pushed that guilt down, reminding myself I was doing this for her. I only had to get through three more weeks—doing whatever it took to help Beau—then I'd be able to focus on Poppy while also moving forward with her center.

It was going to be perfect when it all came together, and all the sacrifices would be worth it. Tucking my phone back into my clutch, I replied, "You know, I think I like your idea better. Let's forget about the list and go have fun."

"That's what I'm talking about." The small lines by the corners of his eyes creased and he held his arm out like a proper escort. "Shall we?"

I took a deep breath, trying to tame the smile on my face as I fought the urge to grin like a schoolgirl experiencing her first crush. "We shall." I latched onto his arm, feeling the firm muscle underneath his fairytale-prince suit. My stomach did some fizzy bubble-gurgle thing, but I ignored it and focused on walking as we passed through the hotel entrance and found our way to the gala.

"Are you hungry?" Beau's voice seemed to alert my stomach as it rumbled on cue.

"Yeah, actually, I am." My nose followed the scent of curry and coconut permeating the room. "It smells delicious. Should we track down whatever that smell is?"

"I hope it's edible. The website for this event says all the food is organic, vegan, and locally sourced."

"Don't hate on it." I put my hand up in a stop gesture. "Just because it's healthy doesn't mean it's questionable. I've eaten here many times and the food is always the best part."

"We can try it." He spoke through gritted teeth, "I think I see waiters carrying trays around." Beau stuck his hand up waving at one to get their attention.

The man wove his way to us, and lowered his tray for us to peruse. "Would you care for an hors d'oeuvre?"

"Thank you," I responded, not taking my eyes off the spread. Everything looked amazing and I was famished. I resisted the temptation to take several. Instead, I remembered my manners, took one tiny plate and waited for Beau to do the same. After the waiter left, I managed to tame my sudden desire to eat like a hog. I delicately picked up my toothpick between my thumb and forefinger, trying to look as lady-like as I could.

Beau inserted his toothpick between his teeth, scraping off the whole hors d'oeuvre in one sweep. "That's delicious!" he raved, then quickly added, "I might need to grab another. Do you want one more?"

I was so hungry I could have eaten the whole tray, so I eagerly nodded. "Yes, please." He went immediately, and I was left alone to devour this tiny-piece of food-heaven rolled into a ball. My mouth was watering as I opened it, stuffing the whole ball into my mouth but something was wrong!

It wasn't food.

It was horrid.

Like something you'd find on the floor after a zombie invasion!

My hand flew to my mouth as I choked, and my survival instincts tossed the zombie sludge right back out. Now it was on my hand, glued to it like a zombie snail ball that made me want to cry. I fought the tears, jerking my hand frantically, resembling an old-fashioned hand jive. I sent my zombie-snail ball flying across the room, only to plant on some elegant woman's hat. *Oops!*

"Oh, did you want to dance?" Beau's voice seemed to manifest from nowhere, startling me. I didn't dare admit I had been wrong about the food, so I grinned like I had a burning secret in my mouth.

"Yeah, I get so excited I can't hold it in."

"Well, here, eat up and then we can dance." He pushed my new plate of zombie snail sludge at me. "I'm glad I went back right away because these were the last two plates. We totally got lucky."

"Lucky us!" I fake cheered behind gritted teeth, watching Beau down his zombie ball in one swallow, tipping his head way back like it was the most enjoyable thing he'd eaten all year. I only had a second to think while his head was tipped back. I was going to have to eat this zombie ball, jive it away, or hide it.

Oh, I'd kill for a pocket.

Or at least a tiny shoulder genie that could poof one up for me right now.

This dress was like a perfectly fitted sheet with nowhere I could hide a lump like this, even if I had pockets. My eyes fixed on Beau, chewing with his eyes closed, giving me one more second to brainstorm. I went with the only thing I could come up with and stuffed it in my bra, right between the girls. It went in slick—like baby oil—and luckily it stuck perfectly. At least snail glue was good for something—all evidence was gone.

"Are you ready to dance?" Beau held out his hand, prepared to pull me to the dance floor. Placing one hand inside his palm, I stepped forward and started to groove to the up-tempo beat with my other hand as we shimmied together to the dance floor. It was fun.

Carefree.

Why didn't I do this more often? But right when we took our spots in the center of the floor, the music did one of those ungraceful transitions like the power went out. When it powered back up, we were left with a slow song.

A *really* slooooow song.

A slow song with a sultry voice singing words I would never repeat near my boss. Scanning around the room, I saw partners joining hands and moving in close. Here I was, staring at Beau from a good yard away. He had asked me to dance, and it would be rude to bail now. "Uh, a slow song." I bobbed my head around like it was stuck doing the funky chicken. "Kinda hard to find the beat."

"That's 'cause there ain't one." He took a step closer to me, leaving enough space that I could have sliced my hand through between us, but nothing more. He clearly didn't pass the old junior-high balloon test when he wrapped his arm around my waist, resting his hand on my lower back, securing me in place.

Yep, I was *slooow* dancing with my boss.

I let my eyes float above his head as we were too close for me to look directly at him. "So," I started, but when I couldn't think of anything to say, I let out a whistle so out-of-sync with the music that it made me look like the crazy lady who hears voices in her head.

"Are you nervous?" Beau's expression was so totally cool and unruffled, like we were a casual couple who enjoyed each other's company.

"Uhh—" I dropped my eyes to meet his. Big mistake. Now that we were close, I could see he was better than a *chocolate factory after a week of juice fasting* handsome. "No. Not nervous at all. I do this all the time." My eyes skidded to the side like Amelia Earhart looking for an emergency landing. "I mean, *not this*." My voice screeched as I motioned toward him. "Like dancing close with my boss sort of thing, but you know, enjoying the music. So yeah, totally cool. Why would you ask if I was nervous?"

Why did I just snort like that? Bodily functions can be so full of betrayal.

His lips slid into an easy grin—meaning it looked easy for him to wear it, but it made it gut-wrenching hard for me because he looked even more like a prince. Trying to avoid cursing, I accidentally said, "Craw!" like I was trying to communicate with birds that weren't even there. Then I slammed my face down toward the floor, wincing so hard I thought I'd blown a blood vessel. I was clearly winning the do-everything-to-make-a-fool-of-yourself contest going on in my head.

He didn't seem to notice my oddities, and guided me in a circle around the dance floor so effortlessly I wouldn't be surprised if he'd been floating. "I was a little." His voice pulled me to look at him.

I had forgotten what we had been talking about. "A little what?"

"Nervous."

"You were?" I asked skeptically, cocking my head to the side.

"I was when I got here and was waitin' by myself. I don't usually go to these things, but I knew it was important to you. When I saw you—everything got easier. So, I'm feeling better now that we're together."

Ping.

That was the sound of the word "together" slamming into my heart. Clearly, I was taking it out of context, and not just a little—like way out of the galaxy context—but something about it felt special and it was meant to stand out.

He smiled at me. It was an innocent gesture, but by now I knew the lines of his smile the same as the two-lane road I took home every day. It was comfortable. Inviting. And while it put my mind at ease, it seemed to have a turbulent effect on my heart, powering it up like it was getting ready for a transatlantic flight. Fighting back every urge I had to grasp at my own chest to stop my heart from leaping out, I instead held onto Beau tighter. He responded by pulling me a little closer, causing my toes to curl under.

His eyes—more whiskey tinted than usual—fixed on mine, and this time I didn't fight them. They seemed to burn right into mine, as if their sole job was to ignite a flame in a reserved compartment in my heart. One I hadn't even known had been there until now. Standing in a crowded room, all I saw was him. As we exchanged heated glances, something else was changing.

Chemistry, or attraction, or whatever you call that thing that makes you flush when they were near. Now, the burning sensation kindling in my heart started to feel like oozing . . . drifting down slowly. At first it didn't make sense and I chalked it up to hormones, but it kept creeping further down. I had a pretty good guess as to what it was, and it was a disaster waiting to happen! My spine stiffened as if was being zipped up from the bottom, and before I could break from Beau's firm hold, I felt it.

Plop.

The zombie-snail ball fell out of my gown and landed on the floor between us!

Beau's chuckle was instant. Not knowing what to do, I tossed up a shoulder, and batted my lashes, acting all innocent. Beau's baritone laugh continued to roll out, hooking me to join in. He shot me a look that I swore hinted at adoration. "I had a hankering suspicion you didn't eat that."

"Yep." I sealed my lips up before I leaked out anything else, but I struggled to hold back a giggle with every ounce of strength I had. Thankfully our song was over, and a fast tempo beat blasted out of the speakers. I responded by pushing back from him and jerking my arms like my earlier rendition of funky chicken was now having a seizure. His eyes widened in shock at my spastic motions, but I was too relieved to care. I was never one of those women who had honed an art for dance, or had a signature dance move—let alone an appropriate one—but that wasn't going to stop me from pretending to care about keeping up with the beat. I needed a reason to break away fast from his embrace.

Beau surprised me—though he was laughing hysterically—he copied my moves. I got to see how ridiculous they looked, which sent me into a rush of laughter that brought tears to my eyes. It was absurd and hilarious. I was having the time of my life, and we danced all night in a manner that showed neither one of us had anywhere else we'd rather be. We hadn't spent a moment working, but I was okay with that.

Better than okay. I was *happy*.

Unfortunately it had to end.

We were being corralled with the crowd toward the door and moving painfully slowly with the massive amount of people. Beau accidentally bumped into someone, and I heard him say excuse me. Looking over, my eyes caught sight of the director of the city gardening program. We'd been business acquaintances for years. I was about to introduce Beau to Tim, when they started their own conversation.

"Beau!" Tim reached over, offering Beau a handshake. "I thought that was your ugly face."

Beau shook his hand. "Didn't think I'd run into you here. Guess they let anybody in these days."

"Right?" Tim chuckled. "What have you been up to?"

"Same old trouble, and you?"

"Me too. But, I thought of you the other day because I was over at the junior high. You should see the size of the strawberries they have in those vertical gardens. I think they're going for a world record."

"That's great to hear. Glad it's working for them. I haven't had time to stop by because I've been busy, but now that you've mentioned it, I'll put it on my list."

"You should." Tim pushed his hand forward again. "Well, hey, it was great running into you. Get a hold of me, and I'll take you out on my new fishing boat."

"Will do." The line was parting as we got to the door, and as they waved goodbye, Tim filtered out in the opposite direction.

Befuddled, I halted. Even though it wasn't any of my business, I had to know. "How do you know Tim, and what was all that about a garden?"

"Oh, it's nothing." He waved my question away with a hand gesture. "Tim's a buddy of mine, and he's does these community gardening projects. None of them make any money, but they make people happy, so I support it for him. He was looking for a way to bring the gardens to the schools, and he reached out to me to donate my machinery for some dirt work. I just had a better idea."

"Vertical gardens?"

"Yeah, they are way more efficient—"

"I know that!" I blurted out, so lost, like we were having this conversation backward. I was the expert on green things. I should have been telling him about the benefits of vertical gardening. This was the last thing I had expected to learn about him. I didn't know why it bothered me, but it did.

Maybe it was a huge hint, or wakeup call. I had been totally wrong about him from the start, and even though I had since grown this weird affection for him, it still confused me. "So, can I ask you something?"

"Yeah, sure."

"If this was something you did, how come you never talked about it? I mean, this would totally help your image, aside from other things."

He shook his head, unwilling to hear my suggestion. "I didn't do it for publicity. I did it because I wanted to."

"Right, and I get that, but can you see how it helps your image, and since you've been doing it for years it won't even feel like it's forced."

"I don't know, Cloverbud." He shrugged, unwilling to put the energy in to give me a straight answer, but managed to add, "I live my life. I like to have fun, and I help people when I can. I know most of the things you do are more calculated, but I don't work like that. I can't do things to show face." He pinned me in his direct expression. "Do you know what I mean?"

It was a personal attack. He was hinting that everything I had been doing to help him was all about something for me. I wasn't sure how to read him, but this realization opened a whole new door of curiosity. *What else didn't I know?* As if he could see my angst, he shifted nearer, and his voice came out thick. "I didn't mean to insult you, if that's what you thought."

"I didn't." My voice was soft and I was afraid to continue this conversation. I wasn't sure why I suddenly felt clouded by confusion. I had never had issues speaking my mind before, but something was changing between us. Even though I had no idea what it was, it made me copy his stance and I took a step closer. "So, what other secret green projects are you working on that I don't know about?"

He rolled his lips inward, pausing while he stared down at me, before adding, "You're something else."

"What does that mean?"

"It means, I thought we had agreed to have a good time tonight. So, that's what I did. I had a nice time. I thought you did too, and now we are standing here arguing about business again."

"What are we supposed to be doing?" My words flew out of my mouth so fast I didn't even have time to think. A heavy silence fell into the almost-cleared-out room. His eyes widened; whirls of curiosity blazed back at me.

He didn't waste a beat. "Come with me."

"Huh?" I turned my head, making an arc as I scanned the room, most of the people had cleared out now, as the event was over, and it was past midnight. I started to pull my phone out to check the time, but he reached forward and took it from me.

"Don't look at that. Just for a moment, let go of the time, and your charts, and your lists, and live in the moment."

I had to admit my hand felt empty and craved something to fidget with as I longingly peered at my phone in his hand. "Where do you want to go?"

One corner of his smile rose slightly more than the other, like he was contemplating. "Do you trust me?"

I don't think it was the words that felt weird to me as much as the look in his eyes. It was a valid question from a boss, but everything about his expression told me this had nothing to do with business. I thought about how I had despised him, but then he went along with even the most obnoxious requests I made of him. He didn't fire me when I messed up by blocking his number. Then he saved Poppy, and even came to get me in the middle of the storm after I had been so stubborn with him. Here tonight, he didn't do a thing I had initially wanted to, but something told me it would work out better when we did it his way. "Yeah." I nodded a little timidly at first, but then gradually added more strength to my nod. "I do trust you."

"Then I have a surprise for you." He nudged me forward, and I followed him to the parking lot. "It's your choice. Do you want to take your car, or my scooter?"

He didn't even have to ask; I was grinning from ear to ear. "Definitely the scooter." There was something exciting about two people riding on a vehicle made for one, especially when the man was as handsome as Beau.

Twelve

BEAU

Clover stared wide-eyed at the cozy—but slightly rustic—all-night diner I had driven us to. "I need to get a couple more tetanus shots to go into this place."

This girl was really starting to get my goose. On the one hand, she was stuck up higher than a light pole with all her green theory lists. On the other hand, she got all gussied up in that dress, lookin' finer than a frog's hair. Then acted all cute and innocent, like she didn't know what she was doing when she danced with me. Even a dog knows the difference between being stumbled over and being kicked. I wasn't going to be a game to her, but before I dealt with that, I had to take care of this hankering I had for hashbrowns.

"It's time," –I gave her my best I'm-over-this-playing-around-stuff glare—"we both need to get some proper food in our bellies, and don't you pretend you have no idea what I'm talking about." She remained quiet when she slid off my scooter, so I filled in the silence, "This is my secret midnight snack place. They have the best brown gravy you'll ever try." I held the door open for her, and I tried to pretend I didn't see her wrinkled nose when she got a whiff of frying grease that infused the air.

"Gravy, huh?" Her eyes swept the old diner-style counter and round bar stools before they looked back at me. "I can't even remember the last time I had gravy."

Helping myself to a menu I handed to Clover, I walked forward, saying, "Well, you are in for a treat." I motioned for her to pick a bar stool. She sat, and I bellied up right next to her.

A waitress, who looked like she was out of every fifties-diner-movie scene, complete with a white apron and beehive hairdo, placed two glasses of water in front of us while looking at me. "Good evening, Sunshine. Haven't seen you in a while. I barely recognized you with your new haircut and suit."

"I've been busy."

Her eyes scanned Clover. "Boy, I'd say."

I jerked my thumb toward the lady while I spoke to Clover. "This is Tammy. She's my waitress."

Clover's eyebrow quirked at a humored angle. "Your waitress?"

I was about to respond with a joke, but Tammy cut in, "I've been waiting on this man since he was knee-high."

"Cute." Clover smiled at Tammy.

My voice was even when I let her in on some personal stuff, "My mom worked here as a day cook. I used to come after school to wait for her to get off work." I jerked my head in the direction of the backroom. "They used to have arcade games in the back, and sweet Tammy always donated all her quarters for my entertainment."

"Ah," Clover's voice was soft like she was still absorbing my words. "So, that's where the addiction to arcade games started."

Tammy chuckled, adding, "I was his accomplice."

"If that's the worst thing you ever did," I cut in, "I think you can still sneak by those pearly gates, just fine."

"I can't say it's too bad of a hobby," Tammy said. "I think it probably kept you out of more trouble than it caused."

"I'll stick with that." My stomach growled, reminding me of why I had brought her here. I glanced at Clover and said, "And it's still the best little diner in the city."

"Did you want your usual?" Tammy asked.

"Yes Ma'am," I confirmed.

"Sure thing." She turned to Clover. "And what about you, honey?"

Not having had time to look at the menu, Clover picked it up and glanced at it briefly before handing it back. "I'll have whatever Beau is having."

Tammy leaned in a measure closer to Clover, giving her full attention. "You sure you don't want to find out what that is?"

"I'm fine." She held Tammy's gaze, but her brows twitched, revealing she was having doubts.

Tammy took the menu from Clover and called the order out as she walked away. "Alright then, two smothered hash-browns cooked with extra bacon fat, four eggs fried in bacon fat, fried bacon, and a side of toast with extra butter."

I waited for Clover to voice an opinion about the bacon fat, but she simply shrugged, saying, "It has to be better than those zombie balls."

An instant chuckle sparked from my lips as I knew exactly what she meant. "I'm glad you admit that your idea to eat that food was a bad one."

She giggled, resembling a child who refused to confess to having her hand in the cookie jar. "I only admit it because I got caught."

That left me grinning like a possum. It took us a while to get to this point, but although I'd known her a while now, I felt like I was finally meeting the real Clover. She put on a thick exterior—all guarded and tough—but once she let that down, she wasn't so bad. I was starting to grow fond of the person across from me. I also wanted her to know it when I said, "The food was the only bad part."

That made her flip her flirtin' eyes back on. Actually, she'd hardly put them away all night. They had been beaming away like she had forgotten where her dimmer switch was. "I had a good time too . . ." Her voice was soft and fluffy sounding, reminding me of cotton in the field.

"Alright,"—Tammy swooped in with two hot plates, setting them down. "Anything else you need, just holler."

"Looks good," I complimented. I waited to see if Clover would wrinkle her nose, or say anything, but she dug right in and didn't even fight a pleased grin that sprouted on her lips. I never met a person who could eat these hashbrowns and not love them. "It's good, ain't it?"

"Really good." She hummed out while chewing.

"Now"—I quirked my head in a teasing manner, trying to get a rise out of her— "Can we agree that from now on, I get to pick the food when we eat?"

Her brows dipped defensively. "Just because there was one bad—"

"Two," I spoke over her, fully being playful as I lowered my voice and tacked on, "Remember the bird place?"

"Oh yeah. That was a little bland, wasn't it?" She did her little nose scrunchy thing I was beginning to get used to. "Okay, you are right. You can totally pick the food on our next date—" Her eyes sprang wide like a sinner in church. "I mean—not date. But you know? When we eat for work things."

I should not have taken pleasure in watchin' her fumble over her words, but I had learned more about how she was feelin' in the last ten seconds than I had in the week. Instead of coming to her rescue and saying I knew what she had meant, I stayed silent, wanting to hear what she would accidentally blurt out.

"I mean, this clearly wasn't a date," she added while giving me a strained expression.

I should have agreed, but she wasn't exactly innocent with all her flirting. It was my turn to let her struggle.

I leaned back, straightening my spine as I took a long look at her. "And if it had been a date, what would you have done differently?"

"Well," she started strong, ready to defend herself, but her voice quickly grew hesitant. "Um, well, I'm . . . For a date, I usually." She blew out a large breath, then added, "Well, it doesn't count because I had to get dressed up and stuff because this event was—it was work."

"Right. And you had to dance with me like that. For work?" I trapped her eyes, loving the flushed glow on her cheeks.

"No!" The pink on her cheek instantly washed clean and now she was pale as a ghost. "*You* were dancing with me like that!"

"Look at the pot calling the kettle black." I chuckled, amused by how the queen of being able to talk herself out of situations was all of a sudden backed up on her words.

"Okay, same question," her words came out rushed and she shoved another bit of food in her mouth.

"You are diverting."

"I'm an expert in that, so yes, I am. Answer the question."

"Answer what I would have done differently if this were a date?"

"Yes." I had never heard a more concisely spoken yes in my life than the one she had just quipped. Now, she sat beaming back at me, akin to a student ready to be enlightened.

"Well, for starters, I would have—" I leaned forward, savoring the look of anticipation on her face.

"—Everything alright here?" Tammy popped her head between us as she bustled past.

I had seen Tammy coming, but Clover jumped, almost startling right off her seat. In fact, I had planned on the interruption because there wasn't any way I was going to tell Clover what I would have done on a date. I looked at Tammy. "It's excellent."

"Good. Glad to hear it." She nodded, while grinning at both of us, and then she slipped the receipt on the table. "I'll leave the check right here."

"I reckon that's a good idea." I watched her walk away, and once she was gone, I was slow to look back at Clover. I figured she had been perched on the edge of her seat, and I pretended to be preoccupied with getting my wallet out. I slowly found the right amount of cash. She was still quiet as a mouse when

I finally hooked my eyes back to hers. "I wasn't really gonna tell ya."

Her smile fell, lower than a snake's belly in a wagon. Although, I had meant to flirt, I didn't mean to make her sad, so I did what I had been dying to do all night. "Well, all jokes aside, I've been hunting for a girl who smiles real pretty and likes to have fun. At first, I'd never thought it was you because you seemed like all you knew how to do was make announcements. After seeing this side of you tonight, I think I'd be right set if you'd say yes to going out on a date with me some time, but I won't ask you tonight." I winked at her and tacked on, "Since we are workin' so hard and all."

A new smile graced her lips. This wasn't her flirtin' smile but something sweeter. Her lashes lowered to her plate—which was already half empty—and she dug back into her food and smiled at me between bites. "So, tell me," She started after we ate in comfortable silence for a while. "What other special projects do you have that you haven't told me about?"

I groaned, not wanting this to be about work, but she read my mind and said, "I'm not trying to exploit it. I am curious to learn more about who you really are."

"Well, I have a bunch of projects, but I don't put them on lists. Or social media. I have them up in my head."

Her lips curled into a grin steeped with anticipation. "You aren't going to tell me, are you?" Her voice came out languid, in a direct flirtation, and we hooked eyes, both feeling the chemistry.

I let my eyes slowly trace the lines of her face, knowing she'd be watching me watch her. I figured it would drive her crazy because she was waitin' for me to answer her. If she was gonna flirt with me, then I for sure was gonna give it right back. I swapped my smile for a new one. This one matched her flirtation. "Same question back at you."

"Huh?" Her back straightened, as she seemed to sit taller but kept her gaze fixed on me."

"What secret projects are you working on?"

"Oh." She dropped her eyes back to the table, and grabbed her napkin, dabbing her lips. "I guess the biggest thing I'm working on is that center for Poppy. I actually found a building that I love, and it passed inspection. It's right across from my office, which would be a Godsend. Other than the location, though, it's so stinking cute because it's that old train depot, so it's architecturally beautiful and has a lot of open space and offices."

"I love that building, too." I was surprised she was answering my question so honestly. I had half expected her to divert to somethin' else. "I didn't know they put it up for sale."

"They didn't, really. I have done a lot of work with the city green projects, and I knew some people who kept tabs on it. I asked about it last year, hoping they would give me a deal if I offered programs that would benefit the city. They didn't

want to give it up due to its historical importance. Thanks
to the recent economic woes, they started to consider getting
it off their maintenance list. My contact let me know. It was
perfect timing because that's when I signed the contract with
you."

"That's amazin'," I said, without breaking our eye lock.
"So, is it a done deal?"

"The contract isn't signed because I'm still waiting on my
approval of additional funding, but I'm hoping to make
everything official this week."

"That sounds like a big project. It's admirable that you
would do all that for Poppy."

"I don't think I could not do it. She doesn't have anyone
but me." She let her eyes drift to the side as she seemed to be
in her own daydream now. If she had looked like a horse with
a trotting harness on earlier, that had all changed. From dancing her heart out for hours and ridin' in the dusty wind on my
scooter, she now looked rode hard and put away wet. Lucky
for her, I wasn't fancy—just a country boy at heart—and I
had an affection for things that looked homespun.

After she caught me studying her the second time, she
smiled coyly. "What?" She brushed the side of her cheek. "Do
I have gravy on my face or something?"

"Nah." I quickly replied. "You look beautiful." I clamped
down hard on my lips, hoping that didn't make her feel uncomfortable, but when she fixed her eyes on mine and came

at me with one of those smiles that was so beautiful it hurt, I knew she took my compliment the way I intended.

It was a little compliment, and I could have gone on with more, but I was testin' the water. I wasn't going to rush this. Whatever it was. Clearing my throat to make a change of subject, I stood up and stretched. "It's late. Let me get you home." Her eyes washed over her empty plate, and without a rebuttal she slid off the stool. I waited for her to walk first, and quickly followed her because now I was lookin' forward to the snuggle up on the scooter ride home. I reckoned that scooter wasn't so bad after all.

Thirteen

CLOVER

I rolled into my office an hour late on Monday—something I had never done in my life. Poppy had locked herself in the bathroom, and I had to bribe her with three extra apples to get her to unlock the door.

Now, I was looking forward to phase four of my plan to rescue Beau's image. I had mostly gotten past my embarrassment for flirting with him after he confessed he was going to ask me out. We were clearly on the same page, and it felt good—better than good to have a crush. I sat at my desk and was opening the first of many emails when Charlotte knocked on my open door. "Morning."

"Good morning!" I rang out all cheerily.

"You had a call from Gary this morning." Her voice dropped to a hushed tone. "It sounds like you have an issue with your building contract."

I pulled my hair back behind my ears as I readied myself for business. "Um, that's weird. When I talked to him, he said we were all set. We just needed to hear from the bank."

She offered a raised shoulder and backed out of the door, adding, "Just passing the message that you need to call him."

"Right." I picked up my phone, pressed send on his name, and waited until the third ring for him to answer.

"Clover." His voice sounded like he was pinching his face in the most uncomfortable way, making my gut tighten in fear of what he was going to tell me.

"Hi, Gary. How are you?"

"I'm awfully sorry because I have bad news."

"Okay." I held my breath, but I didn't need to hear what he said, because the inflections in his voice already alluded to the news.

"My supervisor came in this morning and said they had a cash offer on the train depot. They immediately pushed it into a buyer's contract, and it looks like they are settling up this morning."

I sprang to my feet while my words were waiting to find their footing before finally blurting out a solid, "What!"

"I'm sorry. I know you worked tirelessly trying to get the funding secured. I had your back the whole way, but the boss said they want it off the books. They were tired of waiting, and were doubtful your funding would come through. They couldn't refuse—"

"I'll call them." I cut him off, my stomach churning at the thought of all my hard work being for nothing. "If I explain to them how important that building was to my project, they might change their mind."

"It sounds like it's already a done deal." His voice was soft, but not discouraging.

"It's never a done deal." I nervously paced away from my desk, already formulating my persuasion speech to give to this new buyer. "Can you get the buyer's name from your boss for me?"

"Well, that's just the thing—" His voice dropped off at the end like he was coming to a fork in the road and wasn't sure what direction to take.

"What is the thing, Gary?" My voice pitched higher, as all my disappointment had pooled in my throat. "Just tell me."

"It's your client, Beau Tucker."

I turbo blinked, trying to rewind his words so I could hear that again, because I couldn't have heard him correctly. I waited for him to add something, but he didn't. "Why would Beau want my building?"

"He said something about wanting to demolish it and use the space for a private helicopter landing pad."

Wincing like I had just been slapped in the face, I managed to squeak out, "Is that a joke?"

I now understood this was his bad-news voice, as he added, "Sorry."

I sank down on my chair, feeling a wave of lightheadedness wash over me. Vertigo that said I was stupid for trusting Beau with my plan to buy that building, and even stupider for thinking I liked him when he was obviously a rich jerk who took pleasure in squashing everyone in his way.

"Clover." Gary's voice pulled me from my spiral. "I tried hard to get him to wait, but it was already done. I guess it's time to admit it was always too big of a dream."

Nausea rushed up my gut. Beau had been one of the few people to whom I had spilled all plans. He had never uttered a negative word about my goal, and if anything, he encouraged me. I felt foolish now. Not for believing his kind words and encouragement, but for trusting him. "I need to let you go."

"Alright. Well, I'll let you know if I hear anything else."

I ended the call, and my thumb automatically found Beau's number in my phone. My eyes hesitated at his contact information because it was still labeled *Beau*nezer on my phone. It reminded me of what I had always known about Beau. He was a horrible person. He'd always been a horrible person, and he didn't change. He had just done some con artist job thing to make me think that he might possibly have a soul, but I had known the truth all along. My eyes pivoted from Beau's number back to my laptop. I had spent all of my nights, staying up late researching and planning for Poppy's center, and all of those plans were opened in different minimized windows, almost like they were mocking me.

I could find another building, but it was depressing to have to start all over. It meant more time, and I didn't have more time. Lori had only agreed to watch Poppy for a few short weeks. If I didn't have anywhere to take her, social services would step in, and they already said the only option they had was to send her out of town. My hand slid in front of my stomach, and I pushed against the ache that had swelled as I tried to hold back a dry heave.

How could I say goodbye to her?

How could I possibly explain she had to leave the only person who loved her to go somewhere strange? She would never understand. The change in her routine would kill her, and I would die from guilt. I didn't remember falling to the floor, but I was there now, and I keeled over trying to squash the burning in my gut.

The tiny seed of affection for Beau that had been planted in my heart, making me feel lighter and giddy, was instantly scooped out. Now I was left feeling—not sadness, because I had no tears for that jerk—but a deep anger that drove through my veins like it would be the sole fuel source that would drive me to succeed with Poppy's center. I was more determined now than ever. He thought he could sabotage me, but now all I had for him was a deep loathing. I hated myself for ever trying to help that scumbag.

Fourteen

CLOVER

Three weeks later . . .

My pledge to have a new work-life balance had been instantly thwarted the day Beau stole my building. Working tirelessly, I applied for grants and networked at every city event I could, to see what additional funding could be found. No matter how hard I pushed, the door was like a pendulum that slammed back much harder in my face. I started to believe what Gary had said. *Maybe it was too big of a dream?*

As for Beau, that was harder. I finished our thirty-day contract from my office—not stepping foot in the same room with him again. I had Charlotte field all his messages, only speaking to him directly through a few random emails, and if everything went smoothly, I should have my commission check in my bank account today. I wasn't touching it though. That check was still reserved for Poppy's center.

As for the emotional stuff, something had grabbed hold of my heart. On the one hand I felt like the biggest fool because I had known he was a horrible person from the start. On the other hand, I couldn't believe I'd let him con me like that. The worst part was, as hard as I tried to fight it, I couldn't hate him. Worse, the few times I could allow myself to stop working, my mind would drift to the way it felt to be in his arms when we had danced, to how he looked at me when he said he was going to ask me out. I wanted to hate him for being a con artist, but those moments had felt so real.

Was I that stupid?

Sighing like I had been the last girl picked for a prom date, I closed my computer browser, making it officially the start of my weekend. Not that it mattered because I had now managed to merge my weekends right into more workdays with all my time blurred together by a string on constant work.

"Congratulations on your promotion," Charlotte's voice wafted from my office door. "Making partner is a huge deal. Now you can work here forever."

I tripped over my tongue, spewing out, "Ba ha!" I had worked so insanely hard, and earned that promotion, but I didn't think I wanted to work here forever. Then again, I wasn't great at achieving the whole dream thing. I gave her a toothy smile. "Lucky me." Even though I was sarcastic, I did feel like I had dodged a bullet because the raise I received was enough to continue to pay Lori for watching Poppy. I didn't care that I was eating plain rice three days a week for dinner. I would skip dinner all together if it meant I could keep Poppy home.

My thoughts were interrupted by Charlotte, "Do you want me to walk with you to see the new helicopter pad?"

"No thanks," I quipped with my chin down as I tucked my computer into my work bag and searched my desk for my water bottle.

"Construction is supposed to be finished today. I heard Beau's over there now, doing some sort of victory takeoff."

"I'm sure he is," I muttered, not sure why she was torturing me with this knowledge.

"Come on." She held her hand out like she was trying to coax a two-year-old from crossing an intersection. "Let's look at it from the corner, and he won't see us. Then I'll take you out for a drink and we can find some cute wine boy to flirt with."

"I'm not in the mood." I shut off the last of the lights and pulled the door shut behind me. "Thanks for trying to be there for me, but I don't care about his stupid helicopter pad."

"Okay." She lowered her voice as she continued in a tone growing in urgency. "I'm not supposed to tell you this part," her eyes held a sparkle I assumed was amusement when she went on, "but Beau is *here.*"

"What?" I took a reflexive step back, trying to act casual, but I was confused, and maybe getting flustered. I ran my hand over my hair, smoothing it down. "I don't—" My words dropped because we were no longer alone.

Beau stood outside the door, and my eyes washed over his face. I tried to keep a serious expression, until my eyes hooked on the random head of broccoli he was holding. It looked so odd, I found myself wanting to smile. Oh, but I fought it!

I didn't want to talk to Beau, and now I was mad at Charlotte. Her smile spread wide across her face. "I told him to wait for us out here," her voice was rambling now like she was trying to get all her words out before she got into trouble, "and he wanted to surprise you, so I'll let him speak."

When I looked back at Beau, I imagined his face sprouting a long chin like Ebenezer Scrooge. *Oh, and sideburns and a top hat!* That was so going to be my next makeover for him. I willingly pictured all the things as I stubbornly waited for him to speak.

But he didn't speak, instead, he grabbed my hand. The logical part of my brain said to shake it off, then kick him for touching me, but the sensation of his skin contacting mine sent a spark which trailed all the way up my arm, its sole purpose to disable my arm, and my ability to resist him.

He gently tugged on my arm, pulling me forward, and said, "One block."

"No!" I snatched my arm back to my side, but he was sneaky because he had managed to pull me far enough down the block from where I could now see around the corner to his stupid helicopter pad. I don't know why I allowed myself to look. I had avoided this block since I had learned about the demolition. Like passing a car accident my eyes skirted to the side. I half expected my eyes to burn with disgust, but they didn't because there was no helicopter.

The train depot stood with an obvious refreshing of exterior paint and something else . . . My eyes hooked on the sign above the entrance that read: POPPY'S PLACE.

It was *exactly* what I had dreamed for Poppy.

Tears welled up, spilling down my cheeks as I thought about all of the memories that Poppy would create here. A safe haven for her to find friends of similar interests, and above everything, a place for her to belong.

No matter who she turned out to be.

A dream come true . . . that I was now confused about.

Beau walked forward with a country-boy smile on his face, like a ray of sunshine peeking out from storm clouds tasked with making everything brighter.

And it did.

My eyes pulled to his, locking.

I don't know what this sensation was, but it felt amazing. Charlotte silently waved as she turned back down the street, calling out, "See you Monday."

Now Beau and I were alone.

"I bought Poppy a gift." Beau casually said, like it was a dollar store item.

"You did." My voice was oddly calm as I stared back at him. If this crush on Beau I had been denying for weeks wasn't enough to make my knees weak, the fact that he did something extraordinary for Poppy was putting my heart on a cloud. "I was told you bought it for a helicopter pad."

He started to lead the way across the street, then shot a quick glance over his shoulder. "It was a little lie I told to keep you away while I remodeled it for you. I know how stubborn you are, and once you learned what I'd done, I reckoned you'd stay away. I knew you'd make an exception and forgive me once you learned I did it for Poppy."

"I'll always make every exception for Poppy," I said in a whisper, as I had this sort of scared feeling. I hadn't expected to feel this vulnerable, but anything that had to do with Poppy always affected me on a deep level. He flung open the depot door, revealing a newly renovated space, resembling an upscale private school student lounge, with everything from computers to sofas, to a full kitchen. My lips moved but no audible sound came out. All my emotions seemed to pool at the base of my throat, creating a stop for my voice.

"There's somethin' else." He removed a slip of paper from his pocket and nonchalantly passed it to me. "Do you remember when you told me to pick a favorite green charity?"

I kept my eyes low on the paper. "Yeah."

"I talked to my accountants about setting up a special fund for Poppy's Place, and I wanted this to be my special charity."

It was a check with a number packed with six zeros behind it. I laughed, but not because it was funny. It was a release of overwhelming feelings. All he would have had to do was ask me out on a regular date. I would have been putty, but him planning all of these surprises for weeks . . . There wasn't anything anybody could do more than this. I turned back to him, and mustered up the sincerest thing I could, knowing it didn't begin to express what I was truly feeling. "Thank you."

"You're welcome," Beau said softly, but he didn't break my eye lock when he took slow measured steps closing the gap between us. With a teasing twinkle in his eyes, he said, "Did you really believe I was buildin' a helicopter pad after I drove your stupid scooter for weeks?"

"I didn't know." This was one of those moments that seemed to play out in slow motion.

Like I already knew the ending.

The expression on his face told me he already knew the ending too.

We had to live out this part—the best part. The part I didn't even know I was waiting for, and somewhere deep inside, I hoped we'd remember this moment as the start of something and everything.

"I reckoned you'd try to talk to me at least, but you completely avoided me." Beau's voice came out sort of gravely.

"I wasn't avoiding you." I played coy, knowing my facial expression would give my lie away.

"Yeah, you were." he said without flinching. He aligned his face with mine and went on, "I couldn't blame you, though. I had called my contact on the city board of advisors to see if I could help your contract, but they said they were openin' up the building for public bid because your funding likely wasn't coming through. I knew I had to act fast."

"I had no idea." My voice floated out in whisps like I was afraid to breathe.

Not because of the building. Although I was still overwhelmed by this enormous gesture, something else was causing my breath to hitch in my throat.

He pushed the broccoli—that I had forgotten he was holding—toward me. "I got you this, too." He saved me from having to ask why by adding, "Broccoli is classified as a flower, and I figured it would be eco-friendly since you can eat it instead of lettin' it die."

Speechless, because he had found such a thoughtful way to give me a gift that reflected exactly what I loved. I stood frozen as he took another step forward, erasing the rest of the space between us. I lifted my chin, and now we were standing kissing close. "Question for you." He let his teeth play with his bottom lip while he waited for me to answer.

"What?" I could smell his woodsy scent, and I took a deep breath, savoring it.

His deep dreamy eyes glistened down at me. "Do you still think I'm a know-it-all rig pig?"

"Ah, no." My voice was tiny, and I swallowed, feeling a tightness in my throat. "Do you still think I'm a know-it-all hippie with a nose antenna?"

"No." His answer was firm, but slow. "Can I ask you about that date we talked about?"

My breath blew out in a relief. "I honestly didn't think you'd ever ask."

He dipped his head down, aligning his gaze with mine. "Is that a yes?"

"Yes, it's a yes," I rushed to say. We weren't touching, but I could feel the warmth of his body permeate my skin, and it had a melting effect as it moved though my veins. It felt as if the polar ice caps had melted all at once, sending a tsunami force stopping only when it was fully embedded deep into the fibers of my heart.

It sent out a spark that bloomed into a vision where I saw a glimpse of us.

A gilded mirage.

I didn't know the exact details, but when his lips pressed gently against mine, my heart understood that this was the start of *us*.

Epilogue

Six months later . . .

"Okay, keep your eyes covered." Beau led me with one hand, and Poppy with the other. The hard part was getting us both out of the truck, but now we were successfully shuffling one foot in front of the other. I might have tried to peek under my blindfold a few times, but it didn't work. We had just come from this year's Green Business Award banquet where Beau was awarded a Green Sprout Award, which was the award for businesses on their way to being green. I thought I would gloat when this was all over, but in my heart, I knew Beau was the one who had done all of the work. I merely took pictures and put it on social media.

Instead of driving home, Beau declared he had this surprise, and now my heart pattered away, doing that thing it did a lot when Beau was near me. "Give me a hint," I begged for what seemed like the tenth time.

"You have to wait, my dear."

"Beau Tucker," Poppy cut in, "what in Sam Hill is going on?" She giggled, but it wasn't a sound of confusion from not knowing. It sounded like she knew exactly what was going on.

My jaw dropped to the floor at the sound of her perfect southern accent. One thing she was good at was parroting. That was a thing of hers, but this was the first time she had picked up an accent. I emitted one of the deepest belly laughs I have ever felt in my life. It rumbled so hard that I grabbed my stomach.

Beau was laughing too. Not at her, at what it meant for her to even attempt to talk to him. The therapists we had brought into Poppy's Place had done a world of good for her, helping to open her up in a way that school never did. She wasn't healed in any way, but she was clearly thriving.

The laughter died down, and Beau spoke, "Okay ladies, lower your blindfolds."

Poppy was laughing gleefully by the time I got mine past my nose, but I didn't see what she was laughing at. I turned, surveying the field, but all I saw was a bunch of trees. "I don't get it."

"It's my latest project," Beau explained, still trying to snuff out his laughter at Poppy's southern drawl. "It's an orchard." He held his eyes on Poppy, when he tacked on, "an apple orchard, and I bought it for you, and anyone who needs a fresh piece of fruit."

Poppy took off running in between the trees, laughing like she had made up a game. Beau stepped closer to one of the trees, which was obviously dormant as it was late fall. "I loved helping the school with their gardening project so much," he went on, "I tried to think of a way to expand it. It doesn't make a bean of sense to me to let people go hungry when nature gives us food for free. I got the idea for a public orchard for people who need it."

I was awestruck, as he was always thinking about what he could do for Poppy and me, and anyone else in the community who needed help. If there was anyone I had ever grossly misjudged in my life, it was him. He had one of the most caring and open hearts I had ever known.

His eyes landed back on mine, and he held them in pause the way he did when he's about to tease me. I pursed my lips out, waiting for a dig about bird food or something else he thought was hilarious, but that never happened. Instead, his gaze softened, his Adam's apple flexed indicating he was nervous. "I was hopin' we could do our engagement photos here in the spring once the trees are in bloom."

"Engagement?" I squeaked out, stiffening my posture, not unlike I was holding back a cartwheel from the sound of that word. Beau was a traditional guy, who preferred to take our relationship slow. I teased him for being old fashioned, but the truth was, I loved it. Our dating relationship had started off so perfectly, I hadn't dared to even speak of a more permanent commitment.

"Yeah," He rubbed his chin thoughtfully while letting his eyes trace my face. He loved teasing me, as much as I loved teasing him. My heart ramped up; I was dying inside. *Was he about to take a knee?* We'd never talked about marriage, but I knew I'd say yes.

He took a step closer—a slow step that I'm sure he only did to taunt me—and grabbed my hand. Wishing desperately, I had peed at that gas station we had stopped at earlier, I squeezed all my insides, trying to contain my astonishment. "Cloverbud," he said, his voice soft, unlike anything I had ever heard come from his mouth before.

He wasn't teasing.

This was it!

"I love you more than cornbread on Sunday." His eyes sparkled back at me. Most girls might be offended by his comparison, but I understood his affection for cornbread, and he wouldn't say something like that unless he was all in, forever.

"I was thinkin'," he went on, "I reckon, I will be honest with you about my feelings. The truth is, I don't want a biscuit, unless you get half, and I want to ask you to marry me—"

My hand fled to my mouth in total disbelief; this was actually happening to me! As my chin quivered, tears filled my eyes, and I was about to say yes, when he cut me off.

"—*but* you know how I am." He winked, giving my hand a good teasing squeeze. "Anythin' I do, I do *properly*. So, first you must pick out a ring. Once that's done, I'll take care of the rest."

My heart continued to soar. I never thought I could meet a man like Beau, someone who both loved me, and challenged me in the best ways. He was right, I didn't want a biscuit either, unless he got half. My lips curled up sweetly, not holding back on the affection I had for him, about to make my most heartfelt confession ever, "You had me at *broccoli*."

The end.

Thank you for reading Knock, Knock! It's Your Enemy Boss. This is where the story originally ended, but when I rebranded it, I added a whole new bonus scene. Keep reading to see where Beau and Clover are now.

Also, Charlotte has her own book! It's called *'Tis the Season to Get Married,* **and it's already live on Amazon.**
XOXO J.P.

Fifteen

A Year After Marriage

Clover

Wham!

Tripping over something in the entryway, Poppy goes flying forward and narrowly misses slamming her head on the wall.

"Are you okay?" I slide in after her, as I struggle to see over the paper grocery sacks I have balanced in my hands. Poppy's quiet and stares at me, unfazed for the most part, but I'm not.

What happened?

I cut my gaze back at the door.

Sure enough, my blood boils.

The sight of those dirt-crusted boots sitting right in front of the door is enough to send me over the edge. Not only are they dirt-crusted, but it's like my husband marched in fresh oil just so he could drag it across the polished floors of *our* home. Then he leaves them in front of the door like a trap.

And of course, he doesn't seem to notice the never-ending
trail of filth he leaves.

Why would he?

Someone else cleans it. Either I'll to it, or the housekeeper.
Anybody but him. He's not lazy, and he's actually one of the
humblest men I've ever met, but he has this disease where he
doesn't see where he leaves his boots.

Bootitis is what he has.

Yes, that's a real disorder because I say so.

I glare at the boots as they seem to take up an abnormal
amount of space in the foyer. I shove the front door shut. It's
almost like he put his boots there to trip someone on purpose.
With my arms full of grocery bags, and Poppy humming some
little tune in front of me, neither one of us noticed.

She got lucky. She could have easily snapped her neck in
half and died!

I'm seething as I narrow my eyes on the boots, and the mud
seems to swell right before my eyes.

It's toxic filth making my home a dangerous trap!
Don't do it.

Running a hand over my forehead, I try to calm myself
down. I know deep down, this isn't really about the boots.

It is...but it's more than that.

It's about the way my life went from carefully controlled
chaos—every detail thought out because of my job and Poppy—to this hurricane of a man who is spontaneous and

messy. He forgets he's not the only one who lives here, and one of the people who lives here has a disorder where she needs things to be neat for her safety.

Breathing heavily, I step over the boots and head to the kitchen where I drop the bags harder than necessary on the counter and yell out, "Hey, honey, do you *ever* think about what happens after you walk in that door?"

Beau's voice floats from the living room, "Reckin' I walk through the door. Ain't that enough?"

My hands roll into the fists that I struggle not to shake. I'm not a violent person, and he thinks he's funny.

In the year we've been married, I have asked him easily a dozen times to not only clean his boots before he comes in but then put them in the closet so nobody trips on them. It's like he can't hear me when I ask nicely. I guess it needs to be said louder. Marching into the living room, I don't stop until I'm between the TV and him.

"Boots!" I crash out as I snap my fingers back to the foyer. "I've asked you a million times to wipe your feet outside before you come in. You know that's not just dirt. That's bacteria, and all your toxic oil chemicals that I don't need in our home!"

His brows furrow together as his eyes sink in too, like he's about to go cross-eyed. "Honey, it's a little dust. It's not like I tracked in a dead possum."

My blood cooks.

He *knows* I can't stand that dismissive tone. It gets under my skin, and he uses it anyway.

"It's not just the mud!" My voice cracks, sharper than I mean it to. "It's the *message*, okay? It says you don't care. That you expect someone else to fix your mess, and that you also don't care if someone, mainly Poppy, gets hurt, at which she almost just died."

He sits up, and the remote he was holding goes clattering onto the coffee table. "Now hold on—don't go twistin' this into some sermon 'bout me bein' lazy. I bust my back."

My heart thuds so hard.

He doesn't get it.

I know he heard me this time because I'm screaming at the top of my lungs, but he doesn't get it.

I don't think he ever will.

I fold my arms tight, and the words tumble out before I stop them. "Baby, you think money fixes everything. You think because you provide and can afford a maid, it doesn't matter how careless you are. But I will tell you one thing, one of these days someone will trip over them and break their neck. It could be Poppy or maybe it's me. Then I'm dead. Then what are you going to say?"

Silence rings between us.

I wait for the moment when the light bulb finally goes on for him, and he gets it. Nope, his big jaw tightens. "Cloverbud'," he says slowly, his accent thick, "you're makin' a mountain outta a molehill. Boots aren't going to kill you."

The denial and the unwillingness to even try to compromise flips a switch in me. The anger I've been holding back comes spilling out. "Okay, maybe this doesn't matter to you," I shoot back. "I'm the one managing everything at home. It's not just me I have to care about. I take care of Poppy too, and that's a whole other person I have to be concerned about. It's a lot when I have to remind a grown man what to do with his boots, when it's a simple task a preschooler can do."

The second I say it, regret twists in my gut.

He's not going to respond well to that.

His eyes harden, as his nostrils flare out. I'm not exaggerating, the floor tilts beneath us when he stands...

Sixteen

BEAU

I didn't mean for her words to gut me like that, but woo-wee, that lit me up like a firecracker.

Managing me like I'm another mess to clean up after. I've been called a lot of things in my life, but I'm not gonna sit here in my own house and let my wife talk to me like I'm a toddler. I stand up so fast.

"Now wait just a tootin' minute," my voice rasps. The kind of tone that always makes the boys at the yard stand in line. But she has the audacity to glare back at me with those blazing eyes, like I'm not her sweet, lovable husband, but some enemy she needs to defeat.

A slow burn starts in my neck and flows up to my ears. "You think I'm out there playin' in the mud all day?" I snap, stepping toward her. "I run half this county on pipelines. I'm up at dawn, home after dark, and every nickel that keeps the lights on, keeps your sister cared for, and keeps us in this house, it's comin' straight outta the calluses on my hands. But you wanna act like I waltz around while you clean up after me?"

Her mouth opens and closes. For a second, I think she's going to apologize, but nope.

"You don't listen!" she fires back as her arms fly in front of her like she's having a medical emergency. "That's all I'm asking! To be heard. To feel like you care about the things that matter to me. But you brush me off with your jokes and your boots and your—your *reckin' it ain't nothin'* attitude, and I can't live like that!"

That stings worse than any busted knuckle I've ever had.

I drag a hand over my face, trying to tamp down the fire in my chest. But the more I try, the hotter it burns. "Boots, Clover. We're fightin' 'bout boots. Not somebody cheating or me losin' the company. Those would be something to argue about. Nope. You are yelling about *boots.* And you're hollerin' like I done betrayed you."

Her face twists, like I confirmed every fear she had.

I can't stand it.

She's looking at me like I'm her enemy. I've seen that look before when we started working together, and she was the tree-huggin' hippie out to prove me evil. I thought we'd buried that battlefield.

I guess not.

So, I do the only thing I know to do with my pride and my heart both on fire. I stomp over to the foyer, grab my boots off the floor, clutch 'em like they'll prove some point, and shove my hat on my head. "Reckin' I'll sleep at the shop tonight," I mutter. Before she can say another word, I walk out the door and give it a nice healthy slam behind me.

Seventeen

CLOVER

The slam of the door rattles through me long after the echo fades. That wasn't what I wanted, and now I stand in the middle of the living room, alone.

Why did I crash out like that?

It wasn't fair, but somehow the words flew out, and I couldn't stop them. Now I pace back to the kitchen, feeling so guilty. Behind me, a glass clinks. Poppy's in the kitchen, pouring herself a glass of milk, humming softly, calm as ever. Like she didn't even notice the epic crash out I had. She never notices or at least if she does, she doesn't react.

She's forever wrapped up in her world.

That's the thing that scares me most.

She didn't notice the boots.

She didn't think to double-check because the doorway is usually clear for her, or I'm looking out for her. My arms were full of groceries, and I didn't have time to look. Sure, she's fine, but what if she wasn't? Accidents happen all the time, and there's no reason in the world that needed to happen because I've asked Beau to put his boots away.

"Poppy, are you okay?" I ask, my tone is a little too tight.

She drinks her milk without looking over at me. It's not avoidance. That's how she is. She doesn't need to say anything for me to know what really happened.

I went too far.

But why?

That wasn't the first time he left his boots there. Why did it push me over the edge today?

Sinking onto a chair at the center island, my hand pressed against the counter. It's like I get a bird's-eye view of myself screaming at him about boots when all he wanted was to come home, sit down, and enjoy his family.

Poppy sets her glass on the counter and leaves it there, before walking away without acknowledging me. There was a time when seeing her get her own glass of milk was a victory. That was a huge enough goal, and I don't care about the glass she left behind. I'm so proud she can get a drink by herself, but today I stare at the empty glass feeling defeated.

My outburst isn't about the boots.

My heart pumps so hard in my chest like I'm afraid of something.

Then it hits me hard.

I'm afraid of something else terrible happening that could unravel my sister's delicate balance.

Poppy and I survived a lot these last few years. I still can't believe I'm the sole caretaker for my sister. I miss my mom so dearly, and I know she does too. I'm so grateful I get to be here for her, but deep down, I'm terrified that something will happen to me, and I won't be able to be here for her to "move the boots out of the way" so she doesn't kill herself.

Beau didn't see that part.

Hot tears push on the backs of my eyes as I'm seeing things so much clearer than I ever have.

Or maybe I haven't let him see it.

But why am I scared to do that?

Under the panic, there's a tug in my heart, bringing up the memory of how perfectly his hand rests on my lower back when we hug. It's simple, but I've always known it's a sign we're meant to be together.

He's not my enemy.

We are two stubborn people. That's all.

This time, I owe him an apology.

Eighteen

BEAU

I'm not even five miles down the road before my chest starts itchin'. Not the kind of itch you scratch, but the kind that eats you from the inside 'cause you know you've done wrong.

"Shoot," I mutter as I rub a hand over my scruffy chin.

I'd left Clover standin' there in a house we swore would be ours, not mine. And I walked out like a coward.

With a heavy sigh, I jerk on the steering wheel, pulling my truck on the shoulder, so I can whip around and drive home. By the time I pull back in the driveway, the lights glow soft in the windows. My chest is tight, but I grab those boots off the floorboard where they landed when I chucked them in my truck, and I carry them inside.

She glances up from her spot at the kitchen island the second the door opens. "I'm sorry," we both blurt at the same time.

We freeze and then chuckle softly. I set the boots down gently, like maybe if I handled 'em right this time, I could undo the storm they kicked up.

"Clover'," I start with my voice rough, "I don't mean to make light of the things you carry. I know they're heavy. Heavier than most folks'll ever understand. I just..." I shake my head, swallowing hard. "I'm not good with words like you are. I joke. I fuss. I run my mouth. But I hear you. I do."

She presses her lips together, and then whispers, "And I don't mean to treat you like one more thing I have to manage. You're not. You're my husband. And I'm realizing I'm just scared of losing control, but that's not your fault. It's just... me."

Something cracks clean through me.

I close the distance between us in four big strides and cup her beautiful face in my hands. "I'm going to be better. I'm sorry."

Her breath hitches. "I'm going to be better too."

We don't need a lot to work this one out, because I can see in her eyes that she's ready to move on to the kissing part, and I am too. I lower my face to meet her lips, and she kisses me back. When we break apart, we both chuckle as it seems we are on the same page again. *The boots don't really matter.* She needs to feel seen, and heard, and I'm going to do what it takes to make sure that happens.

I'll leave my boots on the porch!

Maid for My Billionaire Boss

Atalie

"Your work history on your résumé is blank, Ms. Pearson."
The woman who identified herself as *the* Mrs. Michael peered
over her on-trend glasses while she held my paper like it was
an annoying utility bill. I marveled at the way her hair layered
in puffed curls, overlapping like a perfectly plotted patchwork
quilt on the top of her head. She definitely had her own
ozone hole trailing behind her like a sluggish halo from the
amount of product she had used to shellac her hair helmet in
place. "Forgive me for being so blunt, but what do you do for
money?"

My voice snagged in the back of my throat, which aston-
ished me because I had never found a word I didn't love to
express. However, I still didn't know how to explain to myself
the recent oddities of my life. When I didn't respond, she

lowered her brows, and continued, "My apologies. That was terribly rude, but I'm trying to get an understanding of what skills you have."

"I thought it was an entry-level job." I managed in a reluctant defense because the truth of why my résumé was blank was far too impossible to explain. Worse than trying to explain differential equations, and it's not even like I knew what those were.

"Well, it is, but it isn't." She set my résumé d own on her desk. "Cleaning isn't hard, but Trey does have many valuable items in the home—in addition to a rare art collection—so I need character references." She rotated her swivel chair square with my own. "You want to work for one of the richest men in the city and gave me nothing about your life. No people to call or businesses to reference. This doesn't give me much to go on for such a delicate job posting."

I deadpanned, wondering how a simple job interview could make me feel like I'd broken a law. "I assure you, ma'am, that is all I have."

Motioning to the stack of papers next to her, she went on, "I've had so many applicants for this job that I could never interview them all, but I can sort them into two piles." She flipped one over and read, "College student. Fashion major. No jobs. Hobbies: going to the beach." She flicked her eyes back to mine. "She's not applying for a job to clean a house if you know what I mean." She reached out in the most graceful manner until her arm hovered over the trash can and gingerly dropped the résumé.

Then she returned to the résumé pile and grabbed the next one. "Thirty years of experience in house management and a full list of references. Mom of five. Grandmother of three." A pleased grin spread on her face, and she neatly set that résumé back in the pile. "She sounds lovely, and I'll have to call her."

Retrieving my résumé, she flashed it at me. In a voice so hushed it hinted at an enchantment like a narrator of a children's storybook, she said, "There's a story here you aren't telling me." She crossed her arms loosely in front of her on the surface of her desk and leaned forward in anticipation.

I let out a secret groan, then grimaced when my secret groan hadn't exactly been a silent one. My eyes skirted the room, pining for the exit. At this point, she obviously wasn't giving me the job, which grated my nerves because I really needed money—*yesterday!* With only thirty-seven bucks left in my bank account— add to that the way she looked at me—I panicked and blurted out, "I was married." My words came out all on top of one another, making my reply sound like a single, long word.

She tilted her head a-hungry-for-details measure. "Divorced?"

My heart wildly revolted at the mere suggestion of my departed love divorcing me. An illegal interview question on so many levels, but everything about her told me she wasn't afraid to get personal. I wasn't trying to be secretive, and I was aware of how shady a blank application looked. I was one of those people who had life experience and not job experience. I didn't know how to put School of Hard Knocks on paper. Hiding my gaze in the shield of my lap, I replied, "No, ma'am. He passed last year. We managed an art studio together. If you're worried about the art collection, it would be in good hands with me."

"I'm sorry about your loss." Her voice was small but not quiet. In an odd way, I felt like she was confirming something she had already guessed. "So, it's just you?"

"I have a son." Blindsided by how hard this felt to say, I forced myself to bravely let my eyes hit hers again. "He's eight and, to be honest . . ." I sucked in a deep breath as I felt my eyes start to sting. "I applied for this position because I was hoping I could bring him with me to work. He's no trouble. I promise you won't even notice him. If anything, I'll get done faster because he's a big help."

Her lips pinched in an untelling way before she reached her arm forward, offering a handshake, and said, "You're hired."

My head jolted. "I-I am?"

A spark of victory twinkled in her eye before she spoke in her enchanted narrator voice, "Years ago, I was a single mom who had to start over with a résumé exactly like this one." Her lips curled into a coy smile. "I knew there was a story here. Forgive me if that seemed derogatory, but I didn't think I could pass your application up if I hadn't known the truth."

I blinked back a tear and quietly nodded, unable to add anything about this uncanny coincidence.

Mrs. Michael switched back to her business tone, pulled out another sheet of paper, and slid it across the desk to me. "This is our nondisclosure agreement. Before I can proceed with telling you about the job and salary, and giving you a tour of the home, I need you to sign on the Xs." She slid her French-manicured finger to the first line. She held a pen out to me with her free hand. I had wanted to ask some questions, but the way she hovered her finger on the X told me I wasn't allowed to ask any until after I'd signed the confidentiality agreement. I obediently took the pen and signed on all the lines and set her pen neatly next to the sheet.

"Wonderful." As soon as the word was out of her mouth, she snatched the sheet and dropped it into a file folder. As she stood, she said, "I'll give you a tour of the house now."

She led the way out of her office down the hall, her heels clicking on the wood floors. "This week Trey is in the process of closing his West Coast office but starting next week, he will be working out of his home office full time. To start, you can work full time since the home has been empty for so long and needs more care. Once the home is up to shape, you only need to come as needed but the salary will stay the same." Stopping in front of a room at the end of the hall, she turned back to me as she pushed the door open. "This is his private office. You should try your best to clean it regularly, and I would prefer you start in here first thing Monday."

I followed her inside what seemed like a modest office. I could tell by the bare shelves lining the wall, he hardly spent time here. Mrs. Michael ran her hand along one of the shelves, adding a film to her finger. Giving me a wrinkled nose grin, she firmly stated. "This needs a good scrub." She retrieved a tissue from a nearby box, wiped her finger off, and tossed it into the trash can. When she turned back to me, the only photo on the shelf caught her eye. "Oh, here's a photo of Trey and me." She grabbed it, flashing it in my direction. "You can at least see what he looks like since you can't meet him today."

Glancing in the direction of the frame, I expected to see a man who matched her in poise. The face smiling back at me was young—obviously physically fit and demurely handsome. I immediately assumed Mrs. Michael must have been the one to bring money into their marriage because there was no way this arrangement would work any other way. She was still beaming back at me, holding the frame like she was expecting me to comment. I closed my stunned jaw. "Uh, lovely couple."

"Excuse me?" Her brow flattened. "Trey is my son."

My mouth made a silent oh, while I sucked in an extra breath, and wondered how I was going to take my clumsy foot out of my mouth. Deciding flattery was prime, I was about to tell her there was no way that a grown man could ever be her son because she didn't look a day over thirty-five, but she broke the silence by inserting her own laughter, and said, "Oh my." She pressed a flattened palm against her chest. "Pardon me for not being clearer. I had assumed you knew who Trey was. Many of the applicants applied simply because they wanted to meet him. That's why I did the interviews for him." She put the frame back on the shelf, and with a smile still dimpling her cheek, she asked, "You must not be from around here, are you?"

"No, I relocated last week."

"Welcome to the area." Her eyes steadied on me in a way that was more piercing than comfortable. "What brings you here?"

Before I could hold back, I found my words escaping. "I inherited my mother-in-law's house here on Long Island. I wanted to . . ." *Breathe again* is what I felt like saying, but I didn't want to get *that* personal. *Nor did I want to tell her I had been homeless.* I wagged my head, trying to fill in my broken words with something. "Try something different. I'll admit we've had a hard year, but now we're ready for an adventure."

"That sounds lovely, and having been in your situation before, I would have to agree that you are doing the right thing." Her words were soft and warm, like everybody's favorite Southern grandma. Then she put on a polite smile, walking forward. "Let's get back to the tour. So, you may think this house is modest for a man like Trey. This is the home he grew up in, and I've long since moved into a new condo. However, Trey has always held on to it because of the sentimental elements." She chatted as she strolled through the long hall. I was eager to get over the personal talk, so I willingly followed her through all the nooks of the home.

We reached the end of the upstairs hall, where the natural lighting dimmed, and the ceiling caved into a low slant, creating a little nook. A tiny wooden door—the size of half of a person—perched out of the nook. It looked so quaint that it grabbed my attention. Having done a thorough walkthrough of each room up until this point, where she took great care to tell me each thing I was—and was not—allowed to touch, I figured she'd take me inside the tiny room. However, she breezed right past it. Not wanting to overlook something that would be my responsibility, I slowed my steps. "Do I need to take care of this room?"

She turned around in what appeared to be a slow-motion setting. "Oh, that's the attic." I could tell she was forcing a breezy tone, but her eyes bore a tinge of worry, betraying her. "Actually, that room is private."

My mind flashed to beautiful maidens locked in a round tower and secret children on a diet of rat-poisoned cookies. I was about to scoff at myself for being foolish and blame the secrecy of the attic on it being full of disorganized junk she didn't want me to see, but just as I smiled at her, ready to agree, her eyes narrowed, and her face paled.

"Are you okay?" I asked her, concerned.

"Most definitely." Her voice was too firm to be believable and her eyes still steadied on the little door before finally whisking them back to me. "I'm sure we won't have any issues with anything, will we?"

"I-I, ah, no. Don't think so . . ." My voice trailed off as I had a budding seed of anxiety over what I had gotten into.

Also By J.P Sterling

Christmas Shenanigans (All Standalone)

Mingle All the Way

Tis the Season to Get Married

Let's Not and Sleigh We Did

Hark! The Hot Santa Sings

The Coffee Loft Series (All Standalones)

Pardon My French Press

No More Mr. Chia Guy

Truely, Madly, Steeply Brew

Sweet Hockey RomCom (All Standalones)

The Pucker-Up Pact

Shot Through the Heart

All I Need is my Glove

Till Sudden Death Do Us Part

Sweet Hockey RomCom Adjacent (Standalone)

Driving Miss Crazy

<ins>Timeless Christmas Tails (All Standalone)</ins>

Have Yourself a Legendary Christmas (Coming November 2026)

<ins>A Modern Fairy Tale Series (All Standalones)</ins>

Royally Rugged

<ins>Love In Charge Series (All Standalones)</ins>

Maid for my Billionaire Boss

Kissed by My Billionaire Boss

Knock, Knock, It's Your Enemy Boss

Marooned with My Celebrity Boss

<ins>A Heart that Dances Series</ins>

Dancing on Broken Ankles

The Stars We See

A Heart that Dances

A Heart that Loves

<ins>Water and Stone Duet</ins>

Ruby in the Water

Lily in the Stone

www.ingramcontent.com/pod-product-compliance
Lightning Source LLC
Chambersburg PA
CBHW050341110726
47899CB00007B/2596